TROUBLE WITH THE FAKE BOYFRIEND

TROUBLE WITH THE FAKE BOYFRIEND

USA TODAY BESTSELLING AUTHOR

HOLLY RENEE

For my family and the sacrifices you make to allow me to follow my dreams—
I love you more than I could ever put in words.

CONTENT WARNING

This book contains depictions of sexually explicit scenes. It contains mature language, themes, and content that may not be suitable for all readers. Reader discretion is advised.

PROLOGUE
BROOKE

Why did weddings make you so damn emotional and/or horny?

Every wedding I had ever been to, I was either ready to fall in love with someone or I was ready to fall into bed with them. Neither one of those things was a good idea, but it didn't matter. No matter how much I pep talked myself before, those same damn feelings hit me like a ton of bricks every time.

And this time?

It was the worst idea possible.

Because for some damn reason, the only person I could see was the man standing across from me.

I was the maid of honor. He was the best man.

I was her best friend, and he was his.

And we lived right next door to each other.

Liam Gentry was gorgeous. Was it weird to call a man gorgeous? Probably, but I didn't care. There was no other way to describe him. Especially today when he was dressed like that. His hair was so dark it was almost black, but somehow still had a golden hue to it that seemed impossible, and it was always pushed back out of his face perfectly. The black suit he wore did nothing to deter me or my libido.

But none of that was what made my stomach tighten when he looked up from his feet to look at me.

It was that fucking smile.

It was perfect of course, everything on him was, but it was the way he used it as a weapon that fucked with my head.

He could turn it on and off without a second thought, and just as soon as you thought you were getting something real from him, he could slide that smile right back into place and make you think you imagined anything that came before it.

This was why I stayed away from Liam Gentry.

Men like him were trouble. I knew that firsthand, and I had no interest in getting my heart broken by him. Not that he ever would.

When Tucker and Liam first moved into the apartment next to us, I had to tell my vagina to calm down as soon as I saw him.

Surely you've heard of love at first sight, but this wasn't that. This was pure lust.

Nothing more and definitely nothing less.

But he shut that crap down before I could even put on my matching bra and panties and make a move.

He wasn't interested in getting involved with "a girl like me." Whatever the hell that meant. I didn't want to marry the guy. I just wanted to see what his penis felt like on my insides.

But maybe he was right.

Being friends with him seemed like a lot smarter decision.

But none of those rational thoughts were helping my irrational lust and the way this damn wedding seemed to push them all back as I stared over at him.

I looked out across the crowd as our best friends recited their vows to each other. Surely, there had to be someone else here that I could use to take the edge off with to get Liam out of my head.

Because it had been a while.

A good long while and that apparently was a huge mistake.

Colossal.

Because Liam never looked as good as he did today, and I was having to have a silent discussion with my vagina about how she couldn't have him.

I looked through Tucker's other friends. Jase was hot as hell. I knew from the moment I saw him that he would be hot, dirty sex, but I also knew the moment I saw Sophie look at him that he was completely off limits.

There was also Ryan, but I barely knew the guy. And even though I was self-aware enough to know how bad a decision it was to sleep with a guy I barely knew at my best friend's wedding, I was also aware that a guy I barely knew was a better decision than Liam.

Ryan was good looking. He was more than good looking actually. His blond hair hung in his face in a way that made your fingers itch to slowly push it back, and I had no doubt it was intentional. Ryan always had a killer tan and shit-eating grin, and I would bet good money that he was a stellar lay.

He looked fun, playful, and nothing like his friend that

stood beside him with a chip on his shoulder that he tried not to let anyone see.

Everyone started cheering around me, and I pulled my gaze away from Ryan to whistle for my best friends as they kissed. They were perfect for each other, and I couldn't have been happier for Kennedy.

I handed her bouquet to her as she grinned at me with the biggest smile I had ever seen on her face then she took off down the aisle with the man of her dreams.

I wrapped my arm in Jase's as he led me back down the aisle, but I made sure to smile over at Ryan before I did so.

He looked a little shocked by the flirt, but he smiled back.

The reception was a whirlwind of activity and being shoved in different directions by the wedding planner, and it wasn't until I finally got to take a deep breath at the bar and grab a glass of champagne that I finally got a moment alone with Ryan.

"Ryan, has anyone told you how handsome you look tonight?"

He looked up at me from his beer, and by the way he didn't answer immediately, I wasn't sure if he realized that I was talking to him.

"Other than Tucker's mom, nope." He chuckled, and the sound was endearing. How had I not noticed that before?

"Well, I'm here to tell you." I tipped my champagne flute in his direction. "That you clean up well."

He seemed a bit surprised at my words, and I couldn't say that I blamed him. Ryan and I had only spoken a handful of words to each other before, and they definitely didn't sound anything like the ones that just left my mouth.

"I would say the same to you." His eyes roamed down my

body and over my bridesmaid's dress that fit me like a second skin. "But you always look beautiful."

I ran my finger down the lapel of his suit, and he tracked the movement inch by inch.

"You're sweet."

He took a step closer to me, almost unnoticeably so, but I noticed.

Apparently, so did Liam.

"Weddings wear me out." He saddled up next to Ryan, and Ryan pulled his attention away from me to look at his friend. "Anyone up for a shot?"

He didn't wait for either of us to answer. Instead, he ordered three shots of tequila from the bartender and thanked him as he quickly poured the shots.

Liam handed the first shot to Ryan before turning to me with a shot in each hand. He held the shot out to me and our fingers grazed as the glass slipped from his hand and into mine.

And I hated that a simple touch from him could stir more inside of me than this whole little charade with Ryan.

"To friends." He raised his glass and touched it to mine causing a tiny bit to slosh over on my fingers. His eyes didn't leave mine as he threw the shot back and swallowed it as if it was water.

"Friends." Ryan chuckled softly, and I pulled my attention away from Liam long enough to smile at him before I threw back the liquor that burned my throat.

I set my empty shot glass down on the bar next to Liam just as a new song started playing through the speakers, and I gave Liam my back as I asked Ryan, "Do you want to dance? I feel like dancing!"

Ryan grinned and I could tell he wanted to look to Liam,

but I didn't give him the chance. I took his hand in mine and pulled him to the dance floor. Kennedy and Tucker were dancing with the biggest grins on their faces, and I wrapped my arms around Ryan's shoulders as we began to dance alongside them.

Ryan gripped my hands in his and slowly unlaced my fingers before pushing me away from him and twisting me into a spin. My body hit his with a thud, and I couldn't stop laughing.

"These other boys don't have a thing on me." He wiggled his eyebrows, and I laughed some more as he dipped me.

"Boys? Are you a boy, Ryan?"

"You know what I meant." He rolled his eyes. "I'm a man."

"Don't start beating on your chest now. You're the one who said it."

I wrapped my arms back around his shoulders, and I felt so relaxed with him.

"I have several references that could attest to just how manly I am."

He was still grinning, and I swear it was the easiest damn grin ever, like nothing or no one could make it fall from his face.

"Oh yeah?" I looked around the room. "Are any of those references in this room? Should I start questioning the girls that line up to catch the bouquet, or is this more of a Mrs. Robinson situation?"

"I don't kiss and tell, Brooke. That wouldn't be very gentlemanly of me."

I cocked my head to the side and looked at him. "Good to know."

His smile widened, but his eyes didn't stay on mine for long. Instead, he looked to the bar before looking back at me.

"So what's the deal with you and Liam?" He looked uncomfortable as the words passed his lips.

"There is no deal." I shrugged my shoulders as we continued to dance.

"You sure?" He looked like he didn't believe me.

"I'm absolutely positive." Why the hell were we still talking about Liam. I was trying to get laid here and Liam was a buzzkill.

"Does Liam know that?" He nodded his head toward the bar, and I looked over my shoulder to follow his gaze. "Because it looks like one of my best friends is currently planning my death while we dance."

He was right. Liam was staring daggers at the two of us, and I wasn't sure if he realized it or not, but he was doing absolutely nothing to hide it.

"I don't know what his problem is, but I can assure you that it has absolutely nothing to do with me." I turned back to Ryan and tried to avoid the fact that I could still feel Liam's eyes on me.

Ryan lifted his fingers and tucked a stray piece of hair off my face. "I'd be willing to bet my left nut that it does."

"Only your left?" I moved my body closer to his and ran my fingers through the hair that hung in his forehead. It fell perfectly right back into place.

"Well, I'm pretty attached to both, but I need to at least reserve one for baby making. Could you imagine a world where there wasn't more of this running around?" He motioned to his face, and I had to bite my lip to stop myself from laughing.

"It would be tragic."

"Exactly, and I'm pretty sure Liam's planning to detach both from my body, so." He quickly looked to his left just as Liam stepped up to us. "Hey, bud."

Liam nodded his head in Ryan's direction but didn't return his easy banter. "Can I cut in?" He was staring straight at me.

Ryan started to pull away from me, but I latched on tighter.

"Ryan was actually just telling me his plans for making babies, and I have to tell you, it's a fascinating story."

"That's not exactly true," Ryan started to interrupt me, but I kept talking.

"I'd really like to learn more about it. Raincheck?"

Ryan turned his head away from me and Liam, and I didn't miss the way his body shook with silent laughter. Liam definitely wasn't laughing though. He was just standing there like an asshole staring me down like I was somehow ruining his night.

"Ryan?" Liam said his name through clenched teeth.

"Yeah?"

"I'd suggest you find someone else to make babies with tonight 'cause this isn't fucking happening."

"Who the hell do you think you are?" I narrowed my eyes at him and gripped the back of Ryan's shirt in my fists.

"I asked you to dance." He completely ignored my question and that just served to piss me off more.

"And I said fuck off."

Ryan looked like he wanted to be anywhere but there in the middle of the two of us, but I wasn't about to let him go.

"Brooke." Liam growled my name, but I didn't care. He could take the scowl on his face and his clenched fists and shove them right up his ass. I showed a little interest in someone else and all of the sudden he gave a shit. I didn't think so.

"Liam, is there something you need?" I turned to face him more, but I left my hands on Ryan. "Your friend," I made sure to enunciate the word as I pointed to myself, "is busy flirting with your other friend," I pointed to Ryan, "with the hope of getting laid at this wedding."

"Shit." Ryan said the word under his breath with a soft chuckle.

He stared at me, long and hard, and there was something about his anger toward me that was a bigger aphrodisiac than a wedding could ever dream of being. I rubbed my thighs together to ease the ache that had begun to build there and Liam noticed.

He reached out, wrapping his hand around my upper arm, practically engulfing it, as he leaned toward me. Ryan was still standing in front of me, but Liam didn't care.

His mouth was next to my ear and his words were strained as they caressed my skin. "You and I both know Ryan isn't the one you want to fuck. You either dance with me or I'll deck Ryan and carry your ass off this dance floor."

I turned toward him, our lips only centimeters apart. "You wouldn't dare."

"Test me, sweetheart."

I had no idea what his damn problem was. Was he the official cock block of this wedding or was he just going out of his way to cock block me? Either way, there was no way I was causing a scene at Kennedy's wedding, and with the way Liam was looking at me, I didn't doubt that he would hold true to his word.

"Ryan, I'm going to dance with your boy here, but don't go too far."

Ryan softly laughed as I let my hands fall from him, and I hated how entertaining this whole interaction was for him. "Good luck."

Once Ryan had his back turned, I stormed past Liam, but he grabbed my hand and pulled me to a stop before I could get too far. He pulled me toward him, my chest slamming into his, before he wrapped his arms around my waist and started to move.

I didn't so much as sway my hips.

"What, you can dance with him but you're too good to dance with me?" He was staring down at me, and I was doing everything in my power to avoid his eyes.

"Ryan wasn't an asshole to me. So, yeah."

"I wasn't trying to be an asshole." He sounded sincere, but I didn't care.

"It just comes naturally."

He smiled, that damn smile that I loved and hated, and for the first time since I knew Liam, I wanted to slap that look right off his face.

"Just dance with me, B."

I used to like when he called me that, but tonight it just pissed me off. "Don't call me that. What? Is it too much effort to use my full name?"

His smile got wider and he pushed his thigh against mine to force me to move on the dance floor. "It doesn't stand for Brooke."

Wait, what? "Then what does it stand for?"

"It's not important."

"The hell it isn't."

He wasn't listening to me though. He was lifting my arms and laying them against his chest. I watched as his fingers traced their way back down my skin, and I couldn't remember for a second why I was mad at him when his fingers skimmed over the delicate area just inside my elbow.

My fingers clenched, gripping his shirt, just as one of his hands skated around my body and pressed against the small of my back, forcing my hips against his.

His body began to move, and I had no choice but to move with him or I would have been left a hot mess in the middle of the dance floor. Not that I already wasn't.

It was another reason that Liam was a horrible idea. He made me flustered and irritated, and I didn't like being either of those things.

"Look at us." Liam was looking down at our bodies that were pressed so tight they were practically connected. "We're dancing."

"I'm technically being forced." I scoffed at how easily he could go from being a complete asshole to this. Whatever the hell this was.

"You don't look like you're being forced." He looked around the room. "Everyone is looking over here at us, and they all see how pliable you look in my hands. They all see how easy it was to convince your body to move with mine."

"I swear to God, Liam. You could make an art out of being an asshole."

"Thank you." His grin widened, and I watched his lips like I was somehow glued to their movement.

"It wasn't a compliment."

"You know I'm right." He turned us. His body moving mine with no difficulty.

"And what did they see when they watched me and Ryan dance?" I felt his body stiffen against mine as the words left my mouth. I probably should have regretted saying it, but I didn't. Getting a rise out of him made me feel powerful when I typically felt anything but around him.

"They saw what I did. How uncomfortable you were in his arms."

"I don't know about that." I picked at a small speck of lint off his shoulder. "I actually felt pretty comfortable there, relaxed. Ryan's funny. I bet he'd be fun in bed."

"Is that what you need?" He growled the words low for only me to hear. "To be fucked by someone at this wedding."

This is what I didn't understand. Men. I don't want you but no one else can have you. If I didn't want a guy, he could literally go screw anyone he wanted. I wasn't territorial over things that didn't belong to me.

"It would be a nice perk. I'd hate to waste all that waxing I had to do for this dress on nothing."

His jaw clenched and in a moment of insanity, I reached up and ran my thumb across the sharp edge.

"Ryan seemed like he would have been down for it if you hadn't interrupted us."

"Oh, I bet he would have." He looked out over the crowd as if he was searching for Ryan just to stare him down with all that aggression that was rolling off him.

"You're not the only one who has needs, you know? This little hand of mine" —I drummed my fingers down his neck — "can only do so much."

He snatched my hand in his, catching me off guard, and he stared down at me with a look that said he wanted to kill me. Good. We felt the same.

"I bet this little hand." He lifted my hand to his face and pressed a kiss to the inside of my wrist. "Could do so many things."

I didn't know if it was the kiss, his words, or the way he

spoke them, but my stomach tightened and I couldn't think of anything to say to him in return.

He pressed my hand back against his chest and kept it covered with his as he leaned down and spoke in my ear. "Is that what you need, B? You need me to fuck you and show you exactly what your hands could do?"

God, what was he saying?

Did I want him to fuck me? Um, one-way ticket to pound town for one, please.

But I didn't want his pity or his teasing. If he thought I wasn't capable of getting laid on my own, he had another thing coming.

"I'm sure Ryan could show me." His body stiffened again, and this time I thought he was going to walk away from me. Good. I needed him to walk away and give me a moment to clear my damn head.

But he didn't.

Instead, he gripped my hand in his and led me from the dance floor. I had no idea where he was taking me, and I could barely think, let alone keep up as he took angry steps in the opposite direction of where all the wedding activities were taking place.

"Where are we going?" I called out to him, but he didn't stop. Hell, he didn't even slow down.

He pulled me toward the house, and I swear my chest tightened so hard that I felt like I couldn't breathe. Joking around with Liam was one thing because he had drawn the line in the sand pretty damn clearly. But this? I had no freaking clue what to do with this.

We made it as far as the shadows before Liam pushed me against the house and stared down at me with a heavy breath. He searched my eyes, looking for what, I couldn't be sure. Permission? He had it. Want? It should have been clear as fucking day.

He lifted his hand, and I watched as it made its way toward my face. I expected him to gently touch me or hell, I don't know, pull me into a kiss. But he did neither. His thumb drug across my bottom lip roughly, as if he couldn't take another second of not touching it, as he watched.

"You sure about this, B?"

I nodded my head, the back of it still pressed against the house. I wasn't really sure what I was agreeing to, but I was agreeing anyway.

Liam ran his thumb back down my lip before he lifted my chin with the remainder of his fingers. He was staring down at me, and I couldn't even attempt to read him but suddenly I didn't care. Whatever his reasoning was for tonight, I would deal with the consequences later. I wanted him, badly, and there was nothing but him that could stop this.

He gripped my dress in his hand just above my hip, and I could practically feel the tension rolling off of him from that one small touch alone.

I sucked in a shallow breath as he moved his mouth closer to mine, his grip on my jaw tightening, my grip on reality floating away.

Then his lips pressed against mine gently, in complete contrast to everywhere else he was touching me, and I had to stop myself from begging him for more. When he didn't move, I slipped my tongue from my mouth and licked along the seam of his lips.

It was enough to unhinge him.

His mouth smashed against mine, his hand moved into my hair, and any chance I had of not letting the two of us cross this line went straight out the window. His lips moved against mine, and it took practically no effort on his part to force my lips apart. It was as if my body knew exactly what he wanted, and me and her? We were going to hand it over to him willingly.

I pressed my hips against his, begging for more of him, just as his tongue slid against mine, and I could feel how badly he wanted me. That simple reassurance fueled me. I lifted my hands from his chest, and for the first time since I had met Liam, I let my fingers skim over his skin freely.

I ran them along the edge of his sharp jaw. I dug them into his scalp as he nipped my bottom lip, and I used them to grip his hair and force him closer to me even though neither of us barely had room to breathe.

Breathing wasn't important in that moment though. Not when I was with him.

His hand crawled down my side leaving a trail of goose bumps before he roughly grabbed my hip, and I couldn't stop the soft whimper that left my lips.

"This is a bad idea." He said the words, but he didn't stop. My dress was slipping up my legs as he tightened his hand around the fabric and his mouth was moving along my jaw before he pressed his lips just below my ear.

"I've always had a thing for bad ideas." I was breathless as his teeth drug across my neck.

He kissed along my collarbone, making sure to take the time to run his tongue along the slight dip there, before he continued his way down my chest. He slipped my strap from my shoulder, and deep down I knew I should have been concerned about someone walking around the corner and finding us, but I wasn't.

My nipple pebbled as it met the evening air, and he

leaned back to look as he gently caressed it with his thumb and made me want to come out of my skin. I watched his every move as I attempted to calm my breathing, but then he looked up at me and held my eyes as he lowered his mouth.

The feel of his tongue against my skin had me squirming against him, the feel of his hand practically bruising my hip as he tried to hold in both his restraint and mine had me forcing my hips harder into his. Liam Gentry was a tease. He had been since the moment I met him, and I wasn't sure if I could handle another damn moment of it.

I reached forward, my hand skimming over his groin, and his mouth on my nipple was no longer soft or playful. He reached up, dropping the other strap and my dress fell, the fabric bunching just below my ribs.

"God." He took a small step back to look at me, my breasts completely on display, my shoulders pressed against the house, my hips still searching for his. "You are so damn beautiful."

I smiled at him, but I didn't need his words or admiration. I had been called beautiful by so many men during sex that I was beginning to feel lazy at this point, but I knew that's what they wanted me for. My beauty. My body.

And even if my chest did ache a little at the thought when it came to Liam, I had become used to the idea a long time ago.

He ran his hand from just below my jaw to the center of my chest, and I took that slow, calculated moment to try to clear my head and lock any possible feelings into the vault where they belonged.

His hand stopped right at my ribs, where it tightened before he used it to lift me off the wall and spin me as if I weighed nothing at all. His chest against my bare back, he pushed the stray hairs off my neck before pressing a soft kiss in their place.

He wrapped my hands in his, his practically engulfing mine, before he lifted them and pressed them against the house. The move forced my back to arch, and he only intensified the movement when he lifted my dress above my hips and pulled them further back against him.

I spread my feet apart, giving myself better stability, and I almost died as I stood there in that position waiting for him to touch me.

He ran his hand over my ass, taking his time to trace every curve, and by the time he finally reached the seam of my thighs, I was practically panting. His fingers touched the edge of my panties, and I jolted forward, not quite ready for his touch while simultaneously begging for it.

"How wet are you?" he said into my ear, his body pressing into me, as he teased me along my panties. "Do I need to eat this pussy before I fuck you or are you already ready for me?"

I shook my head, but I didn't know why. What was I saying? No, I didn't need him to put his mouth on me because I was already dripping wet for him, or no, I couldn't live another moment until he did?

His hand finally slipped under the thin fabric of my thong, and my soft moan met his the moment his skin touched mine.

"So fucking wet." He slid his finger over my clit, spreading the moisture as he went before his hand slid out of my panties and I felt like I was going to die.

I felt him shift behind me, and I took a deep breath as I waited for him to slide inside me. But just as my panties slipped to the side, I felt his tongue against my pussy from behind and my hands almost fell from the wall.

If anyone found us right now, there would be no denying what we were doing. There would be no getting out of it, but I didn't want to get out of anything. I never wanted to get out of the way Liam was making my body feel or the way his tongue was moving against my skin like he was starving and I was the only thing that could satisfy his hunger.

"Oh God." I dropped my elbows to the house and pressed my forehead against the cool exterior as I tried to focus on holding myself upright just as his teeth grazed my clit. "Liam." I didn't know why I was saying his name. I didn't want him to stop, but I also knew this entire damn wedding was about to hear me scream if he didn't.

He didn't care though.

He gripped my shaking thighs in his hands and continued to lick me without abandon.

I pressed my mouth against my forearm, and I used my own skin to muffle my cries as my orgasm stormed through my body and my knees began to give out below me.

I didn't need to worry though. Liam caught me, moving his body behind mine, his arm around my waist.

I had barely caught my breath, but I didn't care. I wanted him. All of him. Every bit that he was willing to give.

If his hurried touches and rushed breaths were any indication, he wanted me too.

And there was nothing that made me feel more powerful.

I spun toward him, my shoulders still pressing against the house, and I lifted my dress just above my hips as he watched, entranced. For a moment, I thought he was going to do nothing but stare at me, and I was sure I was a sight. I could feel the flush on my chest and my face from what he had just done to me, and I knew he could see the wild want in my eyes. There was no chance of me hiding it.

He leaned forward, his mouth possessing mine, and even though it wasn't a thought that I wanted to have, I knew that I had never been kissed like this before.

I worked his belt buckle as fast as I could, desperate to get more from him, and the way his fingers were rushing over my skin proved him to be just as eager.

It was the moment I had been waiting for since I first laid eyes on him. I was finally going to fuck Liam out of my system, scratch that itch that had seemed to take over my every thought.

My hand slipped under his slacks, and he breathed my name in a way that made my toes curl as my hand tightened around him.

He started to say something, a plea, begging me to stop, or a declaration of love, I wasn't sure. Because I never got to hear it.

Instead, Liam jerked my hand from his pants like I was burning him. I didn't understand what was happening until Liam forced my dress back down my hips and I heard voices coming around the corner of the house.

Voices that were too close.

Liam took a step back from me, a step that put so much distance between us I could feel the absence of him before he ever moved. I pulled up the top of my dress up just as he spoke.

"What's up, man?" Liam nodded to a guy I had never seen before as he rounded the corner.

They clapped hands and patted each other on the back

all while I stood there with my back against the wall and my heart in my throat.

"I have to head out." The guy's eyes landed on me before he looked back at Liam with a smile on his face. "You enjoy yourself though."

Liam ran his hand over the back of his head, and I swear I had never seen him look so uncomfortable. His friend didn't seem to notice, but I did. I always did.

"Yeah." Liam chuckled but didn't even acknowledge my existence. I was just the girl that he left high and dry, well definitely not dry, like I was nothing more than an easy fuck, and I guess I wasn't. "I'll catch you later."

It took a moment after he walked off before Liam turned back toward me, and I knew before I even saw his face the moment we were having was gone.

If I couldn't still feel the touch of his hands on my skin, I would have thought that I dreamed the whole thing.

He regretted this.

"This was a mistake." He took a step toward me, and I wished I could step back. I wished I could get as far away from him as possible in that moment.

I nodded my head, because he was right. Liam Gentry was a fucking mistake, and I was an idiot for ever thinking differently.

CHAPTER 1
BROOKE

"This fucking sucks."

Kennedy watched me dramatically flop onto her bed as she continued to stuff her belongings into a cardboard box.

"It wouldn't suck so bad if you helped." She threw a roll of packing tape in my direction, and I barely caught it in time before it hit me.

"That's not what I mean and you know it." I pouted because what twenty-eight-year-old woman didn't pout when her best friend and roommate of the last eight years was moving out. "I'm just going to miss you."

"I know." She sighed and looked like she was genuinely conflicted over leaving me to go live with her husband.

God, I loved this girl.

"But it's not like we're not going to see each other all the time. It's just going to be different now."

"I know." I sat up and started building our next box.

Kennedy and I had been inseparable since the day we met. We were complete opposites. If I loved it, she probably hated it and vice versa, but when it came to each other, nothing stood in our way.

When Kennedy met her brand new husband, Tucker, I couldn't have been happier for her. She deserved all the happiness in the world after everything her family had put her through. I just didn't expect that happiness would take her away from me so soon.

I hadn't even realized it until the moment the words *Tucker and I are buying a house* left her lips that Kennedy was my security blanket. A security blanket that was currently being ripped from my fingers.

"We'll see each other tomorrow night for our celebration dinner, but I could meet you for lunch tomorrow if you want."

I chuckled at my best friend and the way she still wanted to coddle me even though we were two grown-ass women. "You don't have to do that. Plus, I doubt I can get out of there long enough to actually sit down and eat lunch."

Kennedy rolled her eyes, and I knew what was coming before she even said it. "I can't wait until you get out of that place. Your boss has become such a bitch."

"Preach." She wasn't telling me anything I didn't already know or anything that the two of us hadn't talked about a hundred times before.

"How much longer until you get to walk out that door with your middle fingers held high?"

"According to my calculations." I tapped my chin like I was studying my numbers. "If I continue to save twenty percent of each paycheck, I can open my own spa in exactly twenty years."

It was a far stretch and we both knew it, but God, that's exactly how it felt. Kennedy and I had sat down together when we first moved into this apartment and wrote down our dreams. Kennedy wanted to be a photographer. Hell, she couldn't be anything else if she tried. It was in her blood. It was who she was.

But me? The only thing that seemed to be in my blood was the DNA of a hot damn mess. I had no damn idea what I wanted to be.

Well, that's not exactly true. I knew that I wanted to be a wife and a mother someday, and I also knew that I never wanted to rely on someone else to take care of me. Ever.

But figuring out what I wanted to do as my career was another beast altogether.

I knew what I loved.

To make women feel one hundred percent beautiful in their own skin. Kennedy told me that I was a natural at it, but I think that was her way of trying to get out of being my guinea pig when I wanted to do her hair and makeup.

So opening my own salon and spa had been the dream ever since that day. It was a hefty dream too.

Did you know how much it cost to open your own spa?

A hell of a lot. And that is a technical term.

When Kennedy and I had looked at what it would cost me, we just half laughed/half cried and tucked this little dream away in my pocket.

But I had been saving ever since.

And even though it didn't seem like much, eight years' worth of savings were starting to add up. I was roughly halfway there, which meant I had at least eight more years working for my miserable boss or finding another job.

"Whenever I win the lottery, I'm going to buy you the best damn spa you can imagine." She was pushing all her weight on top of the box to close it, and I grabbed my tape to help her seal it shut before it busted back open.

"That might be the quicker solution." I laughed as I managed to get her finger stuck under the tape.

"Or you could find you a super-rich husband. No man can pass all that up." She waved her hand in my direction and I rolled my eyes.

"I'm not looking for a sugar daddy."

"Yeah." She nodded her head as she seemed to think. "It would weird me out to date a guy who was too much older than me."

"Why? Tucker doesn't like it when you call him daddy?" I winked and watched as my best friend turned bright red with one simple comment.

"I do not call him daddy." She huffed and I knew I would miss this. Getting my best friend riled up with one simple comment.

"You should try it tonight and see what happens. I bet little Tucker would die of a penis heart attack."

"Don't call his penis little Tucker. That's weird."

"What do you call it then?" I wagged my eyebrows at her as I started stuffing her collection of Converse sneakers into another box.

"Well." She looked away from me, and I paused what I was doing to listen as her voice got quiet. "He doesn't know this, but in my head, I call it Excalibur."

I barked out a laugh, and she tucked her black hair behind her ear with a smile on her face. "You. Do. Not."

"Yeah." She nodded her head. "You know, because it's a legendary sword." She couldn't control her laugh. "He would die if he knew, right?"

I couldn't stop laughing. "Yes. He would die. Please,

Lord." I looked to the sky. "If you love me at all, let me be there when and if he ever finds out."

"Whatever." She shoved my shoulder and grabbed another box. "I think it's a cute name."

"What's a cute name?"

We both screamed at the sound of Tucker's voice at her doorway, then broke into hysterical laughter.

"Don't scare us like that." Kennedy held her hand against her chest as she made her way over to her husband and pressed a soft kiss against his lips.

"I didn't mean to scare you. You two seem jumpy. What were you talking about anyway?" He wrapped his arms around Kennedy's shoulders and pulled her closer to him. It was one of the things I loved about him. He never seemed to be able to get enough of my best friend.

"Kennedy was telling me the name of your penis."

Kennedy's sharp intake of breath made me grin harder. She was going to kill me, but it would be a death I would enjoy if I got to see the look on Tucker's face first.

"You've named my penis and haven't told me?" He grinned and I could tell by the look on his face that he thought the name was going to be something like womb raider or weapon of ass destruction.

"No." Kennedy shook her head. Hard. "Brooke's just being an ass."

"She's lying." I dropped two more shoes in the box and began taping it up.

"You know, I was already starting to miss you." Kennedy stared at me with a look that told me she was going to kill me. "But I take it back. Tucker, are you ready to go?"

"What do you call my penis?" He was grinning now as he looked down at her red face.

"It's not important." She shook her head.

"It's my penis. I think it's important."

I snorted at that, but neither of them were paying any attention to me anymore.

"Can we go get some lunch? I'm starving." Kennedy was just trying to change the subject, and we all three knew it. But Tucker was just a sucker enough for her to let her get away with it.

"Alright." He laced his fingers with hers. "Brooke, are you coming with us?"

"Of course, sir." I bowed, and he looked at me like I was crazy.

"Sir?"

"How else should I address the owner of Excalibur? Right, Kennedy?"

She let her head fall against his chest just as, "You named my dick after King Arthur's sword?" left his lips.

I laughed as I slid past them and headed to my room. "Give me five minutes to get ready."

"I hate you." Kennedy's loud words were muffled against her wizard master's chest.

"No. You don't." I shut my bedroom door and smiled. Damn, I was going to miss her.

CHAPTER 2
LIAM

I took a long pull from my beer and wiped the sweat from my brow. Who knew one guy could have so much stuff?

"Did you accumulate all of this since we moved in here?" I stared at my best friend. "I don't remember moving all this shit in."

"It's because you're going to miss me." He smirked. "This shit seems a lot heavier when it's carrying me away from you."

"What the fuck ever." I chuckled, but he wasn't wrong.

I was going to miss him. Not so much that I was going to cry about it or anything, but Tucker was the closest thing I had to a brother.

He always had been.

We saw each other at our restaurant every day anyway. The separation would probably be good for us. Plus, I was kind of excited by the fact that I would be able to jerk off anywhere I wanted without the thought of him walking in on me.

Or fuck on any surface of this apartment without him

telling me that he eats there or to watch out for his toothbrush.

The more I thought about it, the more the freedom sounded amazing.

My phone started buzzing in my pocket, and I pulled it out to see my mom's name flash across the screen. I hadn't taken her last two calls, and I knew she would send a search party out for me if I ignored this one.

"Hey, Mom." I pressed the phone to my ear and leaned against the kitchen counter.

"Oh. Thank God," she said in her dramatic southern accent. "I was starting to get worried."

I rolled my eyes and took another sip of my beer. I loved my mom to death. Honestly, the only other mother that even compared to her was Tucker's. But she was a bit overbearing to say the least.

"I've just been busy. Tucker's moving out today."

"Oh!" She finally sounded excited. "I bet he and Kennedy are so happy. I just absolutely love that girl."

"I know." I nodded my head even though she couldn't see me. "Me too."

"You need to find you a girl like her."

And here we go.

For all the good my mother does, her ability to bring up the fact that it was time for me to settle down with a nice girl in every single conversation we had was almost evil.

I had no interest in settling down with anyone anytime soon, and she had no interest in letting the subject go until I did.

"Their wedding was gorgeous." Tucker overheard her words, and I flipped him off as he chuckled. He had heard this conversation at least a hundred times before. "I can't wait until I get to help plan your wedding."

"I know, Mom." Little did she know that it would be a long-ass time away, if ever.

"I just don't understand why you can't find a nice girl."

Maybe because I wasn't into nice girls. I was into fun girls, if you get my drift.

But I wouldn't be telling her that. She would probably reach through the phone and slap the shit out of me.

"You know I'm not going to be here forever. I'd love to actually be able to spend time with my grandchildren."

I practically spit out my beer. I was used to the settling down conversation, but she was pulling out the big guns today.

"Mom, I'm not having kids anytime soon." I could see Tucker's back shake as he listened to our conversation.

"Oh, Liam." My mother sighed. "I just love you so much, and I want you to find love like me and your father."

She kept talking but I started to drown her out. I was going to be back in Tennessee in less than a week, and I would have to hear this all again then. Hell, I practically had it memorized at this point.

"I saw Katie the other day. She was asking about you."

Katie Hunter.

My high school sweetheart, the one girl who I actually had a serious relationship with, and the last person I wanted my mom to bring up right now.

Katie and I weren't together anymore because we didn't work. In any way. Although I refused to see that fact until she started sleeping with someone else. It was blatantly obvious in hindsight. Despite what my mother wanted, I wasn't going to end up with Katie Hunter or any girl that was anything like her.

"I'm seeing someone," I interrupted her rant about love and happiness and how I could have both with Katie, and I winced soon as the lie left my mouth.

Tucker's head popped up and he looked at me like I had lost my damn mind. I was almost one hundred percent certain that I had, but at least it would maybe get her off my back for half a second.

"Oh my gosh." She was practically squealing in my ear. "When do we get to meet her?"

She asked me the question, but she started talking again before I could answer.

"He said he's met someone, Jim."

I ran my hand down my face as I heard my father's name.

"Mom." I didn't want her to tell everyone. I didn't need my own lie getting out of hand.

"I know." She was still talking to my dad and ignoring me.

"You should bring her to Sam's wedding." She was practically screaming at me now.

My cousin who was two years younger than me and already getting married. Just throwing me straight under the damn bus. It was the reason I would be going back home to Tennessee for a long-ass week with my family.

"I don't know, Mom. I doubt she can get off work with such short notice, but I'll try."

She started to talk again, but I cut her off. "Oh shit, Tucker. Mom, I'm going to have to go. Tucker's trying to carry a dresser all by himself."

He was actually sitting at the kitchen table in front of me watching my Oscar-worthy performance.

"Okay. I love you." She sounded so damn excited, and I actually felt bad. But I couldn't break her heart now by telling her it was a lie.

"I love you too."

Tucker finished his beer and set it down on the table as I clicked my phone off.

"Well, that was an epic fuck up." He was grinning like it was the best thing that had happened to him since the day he married Kennedy.

I looked toward the ceiling and counted to five in my head. "I was just trying to get her off my back."

"And how did that work out for you?" He chuckled, and I swear if he wasn't my best friend, I would deck him.

"She wants me to bring the new love of my life to Sam's wedding."

"How are you going to get out of that?"

"I'm just going to continue to lie and say that she couldn't get off work." I shrugged my shoulders like I had it all figured out.

"You know she's going to want details. What's her name? Where does she work? Do you have any pictures? Does she want kids?"

"Shit." I pushed off the counter and grabbed another beer from the fridge. "I'll have to think about all this and come up with a good cover story. Plus, I'll just pull some chick's picture off the internet."

"You know your mom has Instagram now, right? As soon as you say a name, she's going to be stalking her so hard."

"Fuck." He was right. "You're right. What the hell am I going to do?"

"Pay someone to post a picture of the two of you together and pray it pacifies her." Tucker was full-on enjoying himself now.

"I'm fucked. Aren't I?" My mom wasn't an idiot. She'd have me figured out before I would be able to formulate the next lie in my head. She always had. And she would hate me for lying to her.

"Indeed. It looks like you need to start looking for a Mrs. Gentry before she figures it out and kills you."

"Fuck."

CHAPTER 3
BROOKE

I was already running fifteen minutes late when I opened the door to the restaurant where all my friends were waiting. I had tried to get out of work early, but that seemed to be impossible these days.

I could see Kennedy and Tucker as soon as I stepped through the door, and she waved when she spotted me. Chloe, the manager of Tucker and Liam's restaurant, was sitting next to her. As I rounded the corner, I could see Liam sitting next to Tucker laughing, and even though I typically saw him every day considering our best friends were married and we happened to be next door neighbors, he still made my heart ache a little at the sight of him.

"Hey, guys. Sorry I'm late." I slipped my jacket over the back of the chair and sat down between Liam and Chloe. Exactly where I didn't want to be.

"Your boss being a bitch again?" Liam asked from beside me.

"You nailed it." I pulled the napkin from the table and unfolded it in my lap.

"I don't know why you don't just leave that place. Life's too short for you to be miserable every day."

That was easy for him to say. He worked for himself. Well, and technically Tucker. Plus, he didn't get to have an opinion. Not anymore.

"I can't just leave my job." I looked over at him and gave him a face that hopefully told him to drop it.

He and I had this conversation before. I knew where he stood and he knew where I did. But he thought I should quit anyway. But I didn't have a family like he did. Mine weren't supportive like his. I would have nowhere to land if I failed. Except with Kennedy, and I refused to be a burden to her.

"So," I looked over at my best friend and tried to ignore Liam staring at me, "how was the first night in your new place?"

"It was good." She was grinning ear to ear, and I could only imagine all the places the two of them probably defiled after being cooped up with roommates their whole relationship.

"Where should we not sit when we come over?" Chloe joked as she sipped her water. "The couch, the table, the kitchen sink?"

"I was thinking the same thing." I laughed as Kennedy rolled her eyes.

"Great minds." Chloe tapped her temple.

"Don't be a hater." Kennedy leaned closer to Tucker, almost unnoticeably, but he instantly wrapped his arm around her.

"I'm not." I pointed to my chest. "If I were you, I'd be screwing everywhere. That's the point of having a husband, right?"

"Not exactly." Tucker chuckled and ran his fingers over Kennedy's shoulder. "But it is a perk."

"A really big perk too." Kennedy wagged her eyebrows playfully, and Liam almost spit out his drink.

"My, my Kennedy. One day living with him and you've already been tainted."

She started to say something back to me but the waiter arrived at our table, and no matter how she acted in private, she would rather die before she let our waiter hear her talk like that.

We all ordered our food, and I could barely keep my attention on ordering because Liam's phone kept buzzing in his pocket.

Repeatedly.

It was probably some girl who he didn't regret.

"Do you need to get that?" I said only to him, but instantly regretted it as soon as the words left my lips.

"No." He shook his head and didn't elaborate. For that, I was thankful.

"It's probably his mom." Tucker chuckled as he slapped Liam on the back. "This fool is up shit creek."

"What did you do?" Kennedy asked the question we were all thinking.

"I didn't do anything."

"Yes. He did." Tucker was grinning, and it only made me want to know what Liam was up to even more.

"What did you do to your mama?" Kennedy wasn't fucking around anymore. She was looking at him sternly, and she was expecting answers. "She's like the sweetest lady ever."

I tried to remember his mom, but the only time I had ever been around her was at Tucker and Kennedy's wedding and Liam sure as hell didn't introduce us. I could barely remember anything at that wedding besides him.

"He lied to her."

Liam held up his hands as Kennedy's mouth opened to scold him. "I didn't lie. Fibbed maybe."

"He told his mom that he has a girlfriend, and he's supposed to be bringing her home to meet the family in exactly," Tucker looked down at his phone, "four days."

I couldn't stop my snort of laughter. Why his mom would even believe that is beyond me. Anyone who knew anything about Liam knew that he wasn't boyfriend material. Hell, he wasn't even second hookup material. From what I knew, you got one ticket to the Liam ride then you were done.

No re-entry.

Unless you were me, of course.

Then you got no entry at all.

"Just tell her the truth." Kennedy was always the rational one.

"Yeah right." Liam ran his fingers through his hair, and there was something about watching him be truly nervous for the first time since I met him that I liked. Way too much. "You should have heard how excited she was when I told her. She's been calling and texting me every day, asking me to bring her. She's even been asking me for a picture so she can see what her grandkids will look like."

"Did you send her one?" Chloe was far too interested in Liam's distress. This was one of the reasons why I loved her.

"Hell no. I was going to send her one off the internet, but knowing her, she'd reverse search it on Google or something to find her."

That would be hilarious. I wish we could all be there to

watch Liam get caught in his lie. He was always calm and so aloof, and I knew it would be one of the best moments of my life to watch him get caught by his own mother.

"Why don't you just take Brooke with you?"

My head shot up in Chloe's direction, and I wasn't sure if I heard her correctly.

"What?" Liam was apparently feeling the exact same way as me.

"That's not a bad idea." Kennedy sat up in the chair as she stared across the table at us. "Brooke could pretend to be your girlfriend for the week. She needs a vacation from work anyway."

"No." I couldn't stop shaking my head. "That's not happening."

"Why not?" I could practically see Chloe rubbing her hands together. "You all are friends, so it wouldn't be awkward, and you know enough about each other that your mom wouldn't suspect a thing."

Except it would be awkward as hell.

It would be the most awkward, horrible week of my life.

But Chloe and Kennedy didn't know that because I didn't tell them what happened at the wedding. I hadn't told anyone.

I preferred to put my head in the sand and pretend like it didn't happen.

"I don't think that's a good idea." Liam said the words, but he looked like he was actually considering it.

Like he thought I would actually agree to something like that.

"Agreed. It's not happening."

"The ultimate bachelor and bachelorette." Chloe pointed back and forth between Liam and I. "I bet the two of you could even kiss in front of them and not be affected at all."

He could. I was absolutely certain about that.

But I wasn't willing to find out whether or not it would affect me. Because I already knew the answer.

"You all have lost your damn minds. I'm not going to Tennessee with Liam to lie to his mama's face in some elaborate scheme because he can't tell her that he's not relationship material."

"Oh, shit." Tucker snickered under his breath, and I couldn't believe that I had just said that out loud.

I looked over at Liam who was now looking at me with a smirk on his face, but I couldn't read it. I could never read him.

"You know what I mean." I rolled my eyes and tried to brush off what I had just said.

"Oh. I got it." He nodded his head.

"When is the last time you were in a relationship?" I asked, trying to prove my point. I didn't know why I allowed it, but one little look from him and he was already under my skin.

"When were you?" He asked the question so nonchalantly, but it hit its mark.

He was right. I hadn't been in a relationship in so long I could barely remember when it was. But I wasn't destined to be an old woman who had no husband and no babies and fourteen puppies because I didn't do cats. I wasn't. It wasn't happening.

"Touché." He was right. Maybe I wasn't relationship material either.

Our waiter interrupted our conversation to set our food in front of us, and I was thankful for the reprieve.

There was no way in hell I would be going home with Liam. Hell, I tried to avoid him at all costs these days.

"I think it'd be good for you to get away for a little while."

I stared at my best friend like she had lost her damn mind. Sure, a week away from the chaos of work sounded heavenly, but not with him.

She and I hadn't talked about anything that had gone down between Liam and I or the lack thereof, but she knew me well enough to know that this wasn't going to happen.

She knew me well enough to know that going home with Liam would not be a good idea for me. He may not have ever wanted anything from me, but I didn't know that I would be able to say the same if I had to spend a week alone with him.

Or maybe I would.

Maybe a week with him would tell my libido and subconscious that wanted to be attracted to him even after everything that happened to calm the hell down.

"Can we drop this and eat?" I looked around the table. At everyone except Liam.

But he was the only one who came to my rescue.

"Yeah. I'm fucking starving."

Men like Liam didn't starve. There were too many people in this world who would be willing to give him anything for him to ever even feel the edge of hunger.

But I was famished and I wasn't going into the lion's den with the only thing that seemed to feed my appetite these days.

I was blond, but I sure as hell wasn't dumb.

CHAPTER 4
LIAM

I had lost my damn mind.

There was no other explanation for it.

It was the only reason I could think of that my hand would be knocking on Brooke's door right now.

I had spent the majority of my night last night lying in bed and thinking about Chloe's idea. Would it be completely stupid and reckless to take Brooke home with me? Absolutely. Did I have any other options? Negative.

I even stalked through Brooke's Instagram last night, careful not to press any damn buttons that would clue her into my investigation. All I needed was for me to like one of her photos from two years ago. Yes. I went back that far.

Brooke was fucking gorgeous. There was absolutely no denying that. She attracted attention everywhere she went. Every man's head turned as she walked by, and for good reason. I was right there with them. She had a body that was sinful.

God sculpted her with the intention of torturing men like me.

And she had been. Torturing me.

Ever since the day I met her.

But as much as Brooke seemed like the girl who wanted nothing but a good time, I knew better. You could see it in her eyes. It was clear as fucking day, and I had no interest in going there with her.

Not again.

I had been there before, and I wasn't in the mood to get my ass kicked by Tucker or Kennedy for that matter when Kennedy's best friend fell for me, and I didn't fall back.

I never fell back.

It was some fucked up part of my DNA. I was sure of it.

It's why I stopped us at the wedding.

Maybe someday it would be different, but I highly doubted it.

Did I want to fuck Brooke? More than I wanted an extra inch on my dick. But wanting to fuck her was not a good enough reason to screw everything else up.

"What are you doing here?" She stood with the door barely cracked open, but I could see that she was wearing a pair of shorts that did nothing to cover her long tan legs.

"I just wanted to come over and check on you."

She immediately knew I was lying.

It wasn't that I didn't want to check on her. It just wasn't the way our friendship functioned. Or what was left of our friendship after we almost fucked it up.

We relied on each other when we needed to, but we never really talked about it.

Hell, come to think of it, we didn't really talk about anything. Not anything that actually mattered.

Not unless it had something to do with Kennedy or Tucker.

"Uh huh." She opened the door a bit more, allowing me to come in, and I was overwhelmed by the smell of her as I stepped into her apartment. It wasn't perfume. At least I didn't think it was. The scent was soft and feminine and fit her perfectly.

"How was work today?" I sat down on her couch and looked around the room. It looked so different in here since Kennedy moved out. I mean, it was almost the same, the furniture, the walls, but almost every hint of Kennedy was gone, and this place was all Brooke now.

"Sucked." She plopped down on the opposite end of the couch and tucked a pillow against her chest.

"That sucks." Obviously. But I couldn't think of anything else to say unless I wanted to blurt out that I really needed her to come home with me and meet my parents.

"What do you want, Liam?" Her fingers were playing with the edge of a pillow as she spoke.

"Who said I wanted anything?"

She wasn't buying my shit. She never really had. She just stared at me with a bored expression on her face and was waiting on me to answer her honestly.

"Okay." I turned on the couch to face her. If I was going to ask this of her, really, truly ask her, then I should at least be man enough to ask her to her face. "I've been thinking a lot about what Chloe said last night, and I think you should come to Tennessee with me."

She seemed shocked those words actually came out of my mouth, and I couldn't blame her because I was surprised myself.

She cocked her head to the side and studied me before replying, "Have you been drinking?"

I chuckled because she looked so damn cute when she

was being so serious. "No. I'm serious. I think it's a great idea."

"A great idea?" She repeated my words back to me as soon as I said them. "You think it's a great idea for me" —she pointed to her chest— "to come home with you?" She flipped her finger around in my direction. "This has got to be a joke."

"It's not." I couldn't stop smiling at her and the face she was making.

"So, you need someone to come home with you." She starts ticking things off on her fingers. "Lie to your parents, pretend to be your girlfriend, and spend a whole week with you without any reprieve, and you really thought I was the girl for the job?"

"Yes?" Now I was starting to second guess my decision to come over here.

"And what's in it for me?" She stretched her legs out in front of her, and I knew that she meant business. But the only thing I could seem to think about at that moment was her long perfect legs and how good they felt in my hands when I was driving her crazy from behind.

"A week vacation in Tennessee. A week away from your job." She didn't look impressed. "Obviously, I will pay for everything."

"Obviously," she said sarcastically.

"If a weeklong vacation is all I needed, I would find myself a temporary sugar daddy." She laughed at her own joke. "You're just going to have to be honest with your mom and actually tell her the truth."

I knew she wouldn't say yes so easily, but I didn't think she would play hardball. I knew the way to her heart.

"What about that building on Main Street? The Marshall building?"

She narrowed her eyes at me, and I knew I was playing with fire. "What about it?"

"You have been eyeing that building for how long now? I heard the other day that it's probably going to be taken off the market soon. They found a buyer."

It was a lie, but it wasn't. When I found out how badly Brooke wanted to buy that old rundown house to open her own salon, I called the current owner just to find out the details, and even though it had been on the market for quite some time, there was suddenly a lot of interest in it due to the revamp of the location. The perfect location. Right downtown located near our restaurant. The foot traffic alone would make the investment worth it.

But I knew that Brooke couldn't afford it right now.

She really never spoke to me about it, but I overheard Kennedy talking about it one day when we walked by. Apparently, even though Brooke had dreamed of that place for as long as she could remember, she never really saw it as a possibility.

Hell, from what Kennedy said, Brooke didn't think she could make her dream of the salon happen even in the shittiest building she could find.

But she could.

And even though I was about to use this offer as ammunition to get what I wanted from her, it was something I had been thinking about almost every day since Kennedy had told us.

But I was a businessman, and buying a building for a girl who I had no interest in other than being friends or fucking was a really bad business decision. But right here, right now, it was all I had.

I could see the disappointment in her eyes even though

she wouldn't admit it out loud. "Do you know what they plan to do with it?"

"I heard that it will be some sort of retail store. Probably some big box store, I would assume."

"Oh." She gently shrugged her shoulders. "It was bound to happen sometime or another."

"It doesn't have to."

"What do you mean by that?"

"We can make a deal. You help me and I can help you."

"So what? I go to your mom's for a week and pretend to be your girlfriend and you're going to purchase me a building? What the hell do you think this is? A scene from *Pretty Woman*?"

I chuckled, but she didn't seem to find it funny. "Not exactly. You come home to my mom's with me for a week, and I'm offering a partnership into your new business."

She watched me, carefully. Too carefully if I'm being honest. I could see her studying me, trying to figure out what my motive was, why I would offer her this. But she wouldn't find it because I didn't have a damn clue myself.

"And if I say no?" She cocked her pretty head to the side. "The offer is off the table?"

"We'll burn that bridge when we get there, but I'm hoping you won't say no. That's not a good start to a partnership." Of course, I wouldn't tell her no. No matter what people thought of me, I wasn't that big of an asshole.

I was just being one right now because I needed her just as badly as she needed me.

"Okay."

"What?" I cupped my hand around my ear to make sure I heard her correctly.

"I said okay."

"Yes!" I didn't hide my relief as I threw myself back on the couch and took my first deep breath since the lie passed through my lips and into my mom's fairy tale wedding planning.

"But..." She held her hand up to stop me. "I have some conditions."

"Conditions. Cool. I can handle some conditions."

"First, no kissing."

And just like that, she rained on my parade.

"I'm a twenty-nine-year-old man bringing home a girl for the first time. My mom's going to expect some kissing."

"You've never brought any girl home?" She sounded shocked, but she shouldn't be. She knew how I was.

"Of course not." I shook off her question easily. "How about I promise not to slip you any tongue?"

God, what I wouldn't do to have my tongue on her again.

"I would suggest that if you want to keep your friend." She pointed down to my dick, and I straightened my pants under her scrutiny and threat.

"What else?"

"We're sleeping in separate beds."

I couldn't help but grin at her rules. Basically, don't touch me or put me in any situation where I might touch you. The line had been drawn in the sand. Got it.

"Anything else?"

"I'll send you a list of road trip snacks, and I expect them all to be in the car waiting on me when I arrive."

"Anything for you, babe," I joked, but she sat up a little straighter.

"That was weird."

"Well, get used to it." I stood from her couch and straightened out the legs of my slacks. "There's going to be a lot more of that weirdness happening over the next week."

"I can't wait." She rolled her eyes.

Come to think of it, I couldn't either.

CHAPTER 5
BROOKE

He had every snack I had asked for in his car and more. He also seemed nervous, and I was eating that crap up.

"Are you scared of your mom? Should I be worried?"

He gave me the side-eye as he merged onto another interstate.

"No. I'm not scared of my mom. My mom is the best. She just has really high expectations for me, is all."

That seemed sweet, really. My mom didn't expect much out of me at all. She had one philosophy in life and that was to use her beauty and the thing between her legs to get ahead in life.

"And what exactly is the story here?" I waved back and forth between us. "We better go in there with it straight or I have a feeling your mom will see right through us."

"Shit. You're right." He looked like he hadn't really thought this out. It was a good damn thing I was here. "We've been dating for two months." He sounded like he was speaking more to himself than to me. "You're madly in love with me, but who could blame you."

I smacked his arm, and he looked shocked as he rubbed it with his opposite hand. "You can't hit the driver."

"Then tell the driver not to be an asshole."

This felt awkward. I had been around Liam too many times to count, but never quite like this and definitely not after what happened. There was always some other element involved, some other friend. If it ever seemed like we were crossing the line, one of our friends would be there to throw us right back into reality.

"Okay, okay. But we do have to pretend to be into each other. My mom's not going to fall for it if you're smacking me or giving me your evil eye the whole time."

"What evil eye?" I acted offended.

"That evil eye." He pointed toward my face. "It scares me enough. I don't need you putting my mom through it too."

I rolled said eyes before looking out the windshield. "So, how did we meet?"

"My mom's seen you before, Brooke." He looked over at me then back at the road. "We met when I moved in next door to you. We need to keep things as close to the truth as possible."

"And then from there?" I looked over at him skeptically. His nonplan was not a plan at all, but this was his rodeo. I was just here for the show.

"We'll play it by ear."

And a show it was going to be.

"And what about your friends? Are we going to see any of them while we're here? What are you going to tell them?"

He scratched at the slight scruff on his face. "We will.

We'll see Jase and Sophie and Ryan and probably a few others from my high school days." I could tell he was thinking long and hard as he slipped his bottom lip between his teeth. He looked so incredibly sexy when he did that, but I had no room for those thoughts anymore. "We should probably just stick with our lie across the board. I don't want to slip up and something happen in front of my parents."

"Okay." I nodded my head. Not only would I be putting on a show for his parents but the whole damn town.

"You can tell Sophie the truth if you want to though. Just tell her to keep it between y'all."

I smiled because he knew Sophie was my girl even if I rarely got to see her. Sophie was Tucker's little sister and the girlfriend to one of his best friends, Jase Hale. Jase was a walking sexual fantasy.

He knew it. She knew it. We all knew it.

And then there was Ryan.

"So let's get these rules straight before we get there." I started ticking them off on my fingers. "No tongue kissing. No sleeping in the same bed. This goes without saying, but no sex."

"Well, this is going to be a fun trip." He chuckled, but I knew we were both on the same page. Those things weren't on the table before, and they definitely weren't on the table now.

"I talked to the owner of the Marshall building, by the way."

"Oh yeah." I don't know why this surprised me so much, but there was something about this entire thing that seemed too good to be true.

The thing I had been wanting for as long as I could remember, the thing no one else besides Kennedy believed I was capable of, was being dangled right in front of my face. And all I had to do was pretend to be his girlfriend for a week?

I'd believe it when I had some sort of contract in my hand. Or you know, the keys to the building.

But if it did happen, and that was a huge if, then Liam was going to be my business partner. I didn't know how involved or how silent of a partner he planned to be, but I knew with one hundred percent certainty that little fact put Liam one more notch up on the don't fucking go there meter.

And he was already pretty high.

"Yeah. I made him an offer just below asking price over the phone, but told him that I'd send the offer in writing when I got to Tennessee."

He already submitted an offer?

I turned in my seat so I was fully facing him. "And what did he say?"

"He said he'd think it over. He seems like a nice old man, but I'm sure he's going to play hardball. Hell, I wouldn't sell it below asking price."

"Then why did you offer below asking? What was the asking anyway?" Because I had no idea if I'd be able to contribute half. I think I'd be close, but once I did that, I'd be completely wiped out. Add water to your shampoo bottle until every trace of soap was gone wiped out.

"Just to give us a little wiggle room for negotiations. I don't want him jumping way above asking if he gets any other offers."

That made sense. Clearly, I had never bought any piece of real estate. "And the price?"

I held my breath as I waited for his answer.

He swallowed, and I knew he didn't want to tell me. Which meant it's probably way more than I could afford.

"I'll worry about the building and you worry about everything else."

Wait. What?

"I can't let you just buy the damn building without me contributing. Then it wouldn't be ours. It would be yours." And there was no way in hell I was going to let that happen.

"No. It wouldn't. It would be in both of our names, fifty-fifty."

"What's in this for you, Liam?" Why the hell would you buy your neighbor who you tongue fucked against the wall of a building like some sort of knight in shining armor and not have any expectations?

"I'm a businessman, Brooke, and I think you're smart. I'm not buying you a building to be some sort of hero. This will be a fifty-fifty partnership, and I think we can make a lot of money."

"You think I'm smart?" Somehow that was the only thing I seemed to hear.

"Of course, I think you're smart." He looked over at me and seemed to study me. Too long while he was driving and definitely too long for my comfort. "I wouldn't offer to go into business with you if I didn't think you were smart enough to make it successful."

Well damn. I wasn't foolish enough to not realize how much those words coming from him affected me. "What about Tucker? Is he going to be in on this too?"

I didn't know if I wanted that or not. Of course, I knew that Liam and Tucker were business partners and best friends, but there was something about the thought that all of this could have been charity from Tucker simply because I'm his wife's best friend that completely turned me off.

"No. It's just me and you." He ran his fingers through his hair as if that small, simple statement made him uncomfortable. "Are you okay with that?"

"Yeah." I nodded my head as I studied his profile. "I'm okay with that." This was a bad idea. I knew it deep down the moment he offered it, but the way I was currently staring at the curve of his bottom lip seemed to reiterate the fact.

Because suddenly I was more worried about remembering the feel of his lips on mine than what it would feel like to have those keys in my hands.

CHAPTER 6
LIAM

Brooke was fast asleep when we pulled up to my parent's house. It was getting dark, and we had been on the road for several hours.

I spent most of the time trying to figure out what the hell I was doing. Brooke spent it with a tiny bit of drool running down her face.

I stared at my childhood home and took a deep breath. Coming home should have been easy. Hell, it was always easy, but I had to go and complicate the hell out of it with my big mouth and my even bigger stupidity.

Brooke started moving next to me, and she blinked her eyes open before looking around with a sweet, lost look on her face. "Are we here?"

"We are." I pulled the keys out of the ignition and tucked them into my pocket.

Brooke stared out the windshield of the car at my home, and I tried to imagine how she was seeing it. The only time she had ever been to Tennessee, she had been to Tucker's parents' house.

And Tucker's house was at least two times the size of my mom and dad's. I didn't come from money. My parents worked their asses off every day to give me the things I wanted and needed, and I didn't really realize until I got older how much of a toll that must have taken on them.

I never appreciated anything the way that I should have.

But my parents never really acknowledged the fact either. I always thought we had just as much as everyone else, even when we didn't

I wasn't embarrassed by the fact, but I just wanted to know what was running through her head.

"You could have stopped at a rest stop." She pulled the mirror down and started fixing her hair. "Your mom's going to think, 'Oh great. Liam brought a hobo home that he found on the side of the road'."

I chuckled. "You do not look like a hobo."

She pulled a small bag out from the much larger one by her feet and started pulling out all sorts of products. She wiped under her eyes where mascara had run then started dabbing some crap in its place.

"You don't need all that. You look beautiful." I wasn't just saying that either. She did look beautiful. She always did.

"I appreciate the sentiment, Liam, but I am not walking into that house to meet your parents for the first time looking like this." She started rubbing gloss on her lips.

If I didn't know any better, I'd say she was at least half as nervous as I was.

"I'm going to start getting the bags out of the trunk." It might take me all night too. That girl could pack.

I pulled our bags from the car and waited as she climbed out of the passenger seat and straightened out her clothes.

She was dressed comfortably for the long drive, and I could tell that it bothered her. I rarely ever saw Brooke not dressed to the nines.

"This way." I nodded toward the front door and grabbed all our bags.

"I can get one of those." She started to reach for one of her bags, but I moved it farther away from her. "So my mom can have my balls first thing? No, thank you." It didn't matter if my mom was here or not. That girl was crazy if she thought I'd let her carry her bags.

She walked behind me, close enough that I could still smell the scent of her perfume, and I hesitated at the front door before pushing it open. "You ready for this?"

"As ready as I'm ever going to be." She shrugged, and I grinned as I stepped through the door.

"Mom?" I set our bags against the wall. "Dad? Where are y'all at?"

My mom came around the corner with a dishrag in her hand and a giant smile on her face. "Jim," she yelled my dad's name. "You owe me money." Then she walked right past me, her only son who she hadn't seen in months, and wrapped Brooke in her arms.

"Liam's dad and I had a little bet about whether or not you were real." She grinned at Brooke and held her at arm's length so she could get a good look at her. "I mean of course you're real, but that you're really dating our son."

Brooke laughed, almost nervously, and I worried that we'd blow it before we even got started.

"It took a lot of convincing on his part." Brooke laughed as my mother smiled.

"Well, come on in." My mom backed out of her way and motioned toward the kitchen. The heart of this house.

As she passed me, she patted my cheek and winked at me, actually winked at me, but I couldn't lie and say it didn't feel good to see her so happy. Even if her happiness was due to my lies.

"Your home is beautiful." Brooke turned in a circle to take in the kitchen and my mom beamed at her compliment.

"Thank you." She walked up to the stove and stirred something that smelled absolutely delicious. "There's about thirty years of work and constant changes. Bless my poor husband."

Right on cue, my dad walked into the room behind me and clapped me on the back. "It's the reason I can never find anything around here. She's always rearranging."

My mom rolled her eyes but still smiled at him with a smile I had seen my entire life. She smiled at him that way every single time she saw him. Even if she was angry, he'd always end up making her smile. "He's just getting old and senile and blaming it on me."

"Son." My dad looked to me for support. He was right, of course, but there was no way in hell I was saying that to her.

"I'm not getting in the middle of this." I crossed my arms and watched Brooke as she watched my family.

"You must be Brooke." My dad made his way across the kitchen and placed a kiss to the top of my mom's head before he pulled Brooke into a hug.

Brooke grinned at me over his shoulder, and I couldn't help smiling back at her with my over-loving parents. "It's nice to meet you, sir."

"Lord, don't call me sir. I'm Jim." He wrapped his arm around her shoulder and turned them both to face me. "Now tell me how my knucklehead of a son over there managed to convince you to date him."

"You two do know that I'm standing right here, right?"

"We know." My dad chuckled before letting Brooke go and grabbing a couple beers out of the fridge. "Brooke?"

"No. I'm good. Thank you."

He tossed one of the beers in my direction without asking.

"Mrs. Gentry, is there anything I can help you with?"

My mom was still stirring something on the stove as she looked up at Brooke. "Oh, no. You just had a long drive. You must be tired. Go relax." She waved her off as she always did. That woman rarely let anyone help her do anything.

"I'm okay." Brooke walked to the sink and started washing her hands. "Just tell me what to do."

My dad raised his eyebrows at me, but I ignored him. I was too busy watching her.

"Well, have you ever made biscuits before?" My mom wiped her hands on her dishtowel before grabbing the flour.

"Not even once." Brooke chuckled but saddled up next to my mom. "But I can learn."

My dad nodded his head toward the door and slipped out before I could say anything.

I watched Brooke and my mom laugh as Brooke sprinkled flour out on the counter and my mom talked about family secrets to making the best biscuits. I absolutely fucking hated it. And not because they seemed to be getting along or that my mom seemed to really like her, but there was some part of me that liked seeing her there.

I walked up behind her and her back straightened as my skin touched hers, but my mom was too busy scooping out more flour to notice. "I'm going to go talk with my dad a bit. You good?"

"She's fine," my mom answered for her as she continued to work.

Brooke nodded her head with a smile on her face. A smile that dropped the moment I pressed my lips against her bare shoulder.

She looked over at me just as I heard the slight uptick of her breath, and there was something about the way she was looking at me through her lashes that suddenly make me want to bend her over the counter without any thought of repercussions.

We hadn't even been here for ten damn minutes, and already she was fucking with my head.

I couldn't help staring at her as I backed out of the kitchen. My mom was talking to her in a soft voice that I couldn't hear, and Brooke was laughing without a second thought of my lips touching her skin.

I needed to get my shit together.

"So, how are things?" My dad leaned back in his old leather chair and stared over at me where I still stood watching Brooke.

I made my way over to the couch and sat down even though the urge to stay right there with her was overpowering. Brooke wasn't going to slip up and say something to my mom. She was smarter than I gave her credit for.

"Everything's good. Both the restaurant and the bar have been busy every night. I have no complaints."

"That's good to hear. You aren't working yourself into the ground, are you?" My dad had been a hard worker all of his life, but one of the things he had instilled in me a long time ago was that all that work wasn't worth a thing if you didn't leave time to live.

"Not too much." I leaned back into the cushion and

relaxed. This place, the feel of it, the smell of it, nothing had ever felt quite like home since leaving here, and there was something about being back here that took a weight off my shoulders. "We've got a pretty damn good team right now."

"Good." My dad nodded his head. "What's next? You all going to take it easy for a while or you already have something else up your sleeve?"

I couldn't tell him about the business proposition I made Brooke. Not only would he either think the business idea or our relationship was a sham, he would lay into me about how dumb of a decision it was.

He would try to talk some sense into me, and I didn't have time for that right now.

"We're working on perfecting what we have for right now."

I never lied to my dad, and I hated that I was doing it now.

"What about that girl in there?" He nodded toward the kitchen.

"What about her?" My heart rate kicked up.

"Is it serious?" He arched an eyebrow at me.

"It's as serious as I get, I guess." My dad knew I wasn't ready to settle down regardless of how badly my mom wanted it. Me and him had talked about it a dozen times.

I told him I would settle down when I was ready, and he told me that being ready had nothing to do with it. According to him, it would knock me off my ass when it was time, and if it didn't? It wasn't time.

"That's a bullshit answer and you know it." He crossed his arms, and even though he was trying to have a stern heart to heart with me, I couldn't help laughing at him. My dad didn't have an ounce of hard-ass in his body.

Not a single trace.

"I haven't been knocked on my ass yet if that's what you're asking."

He nodded his head in understanding. My mom was passionate, full of life, and sometimes overbearing, but my dad was the rational one. They balanced each other out perfectly.

"I have a feeling about that one in there."

"You've met her once and you already have a feeling about her?" My dad was so full of shit.

"Exactly." He stretched back in his recliner like he didn't have a worry in the world. "Sometimes you just know."

"You're crazy." I shook my head. And here I thought he was the level-headed one.

"Think what you want, but I'll be telling you I told you so."

"You're getting worse than Mom in your old age. I think she was right. You are going senile."

He clicked on the TV and whatever football game that was currently playing blasted through the speakers.

"We'll see."

By the time my mom and Brooke finally made their way into the living room, Brooke was covered in flour and a giant smile.

"I made biscuits." She shrugged her shoulders, and I swear if I was some lovesick puppy I would have thought it was the cutest fucking thing I'd ever seen. But I wasn't, I was just pretending to be.

"I see that." I stood from the couch and made my way over to where she stood. "Did you actually put any flour in the biscuits or are you wearing it all?"

She smacked my arm playfully, and God, the urge to press my lips against hers was strong.

What the hell was happening?

"Let's eat." My mom motioned toward the dining room, and we all followed her in there.

Brooke took the seat next to me, and my mom had a grin on her face as she started passing around food.

"Brooke tells me that Kennedy and Tucker finally moved out." She passed me the biscuits, and I had to admit they looked amazing.

"Yeah. Just this week, actually. It's weirdly quiet in my apartment."

"Mine too." Brooke nodded around a bite of food.

She was eating the food so quickly you would think the girl had never had a home-cooked meal in her life.

My mom grinned harder. "Have you two thought about moving in together?"

I coughed around my drink and I was pretty sure Brooke was choking on her biscuit.

"Sarah, leave them alone." My dad shook his head, but he didn't seem at all surprised by her words.

"What? I was just asking. It would save them a lot of money on bills."

And a lot of time on her schedule of marriage and children.

"I just got my own bathroom for the first time in my entire life. I'm not sure I'm ready to share again just yet." Brooke laughed.

I don't know why, but that kind of shocked me.

Brooke and I had never talked about our lives before we met, what our families were like, but I had always assumed that she came from a lot of money like Kennedy.

But maybe I was wrong.

Maybe I didn't know nearly what I thought I knew about her.

"Do you have any siblings?" My mom sounded genuinely interested in learning about her, and I felt like a complete asshole because I was waiting for the answer too.

"No siblings." She shook her head and pushed some food around her plate. "It was just me and my mom."

The way she said it was like it was the worst reality in the world, and maybe for her, it was.

"What was this one like growing up?" She hiked her thumb in my direction, and it was easy to see she was deflecting the conversation off of her and her family.

"He was a bit wild." My mom laughed as she looked at me. "Football star, heartthrob, several broken bones."

I wagged my eyebrows at her as my mom listed off my shining qualities, and she laughed before knocking her knee against mine under the table.

"He was also really bad at English." I swiveled my head in my dad's direction. "It almost got him kicked off the football team a couple times."

"You're supposed to be telling her the positive things, Dad. Not the negative."

"No. I want to hear the negative." She scooted her chair closer to the table and simultaneously closer to me.

"Well, he also had the hardest time learning to talk." My mom looked at me like it was her favorite memory in the world. "He had this little lisp and you could barely understand anything he said."

"Mom." I laid my head back in frustration. I didn't need Brooke knowing all my dirty little secrets or my embarrassing ones.

"It was cute."

"A lot cuter than that time we caught you trying to sneak your girlfriend in." My dad nodded, and I wished he would stop right where he was. I hadn't thought about Katie in years. Hell, I hadn't seen her in years.

Katie was the first and last girl I let break my heart.

"He got caught?" Brooke was laughing.

"Yes. He got caught." My mom looked a lot less pleased with this memory. "He isn't as smooth as he thinks he is."

"No." Brooke shook her head with a smile. "He certainly is not."

"What the hell is that supposed to mean?" I was smooth. I was the smoothest damn thing they had ever seen.

"Nothing." She patted my cheek like I was a child as she fake whispered to my mom. "I can't mess with his ego too much. He gets all whiny."

"Don't I know it." My mom nodded her head in my dad's direction.

"I am not whiny." My dad took my words right out of my mouth.

"Of course you're not, honey." She patted his hand before scooping some more food on his plate and winking at Brooke.

I don't know what it was, but there was something about seeing my mom and Brooke get along so well that did something. I don't even know how to explain it.

This was Brooke. She wasn't acting, there was no pretending, except for her feelings for me. She was who she was, and my mom loved her.

It was a blessing and a huge problem.

A huge fucking problem.

I didn't want to let my mom down more when Brooke

and I "broke up" then I would have if I had just shown up alone.

I was so damn screwed.

I needed Brooke to be less likable.

I didn't need or want my mom to love her.

It would just make everything more difficult.

But it didn't matter what I wanted, my mom was falling for her before my very eyes, and there wasn't much I could do about it.

"I still have to get a dress for the wedding if you'd like to go shopping one day." My mom was looking at Brooke, and I could see all the daughter-in-law fantasies flash through her head.

"I'd love that. I could actually use a new dress too."

Brooke's plate was almost empty so I loaded her up with more mashed potatoes and green beans.

"Thanks." She tucked a piece of hair behind her ear.

"You're welcome."

"Brooke, what do you do?"

She looked up at my dad and shifted in her seat. "I manage a salon."

She said it like it was something she shouldn't be proud of, like what she did wasn't important, and I hated that she felt that way.

"She's planning to open her own salon and spa." I had to go and open my big mouth.

"That's incredible." My mom smiled across the table at her. "I'm sure Liam could be lots of help. He has done a great job with his businesses."

"Yeah." Brooke nodded and smiled over at me. "He's been offering up some good advice."

Please don't say I bribed you with a building.

"Are you wanting to do something in the same downtown area that Rock Bottom is in?" My dad seemed genuinely interested.

Brooke nodded and I could tell from the way her eyes lit up that this was truly what she wanted. I wondered how many people had asked her about her dreams. I wondered how many had ever cared. "There's this old house right in the middle of downtown. It almost seems a bit out of place with all the new construction and remodels going on, but I'd love to buy it and turn it into exactly what I want." She barely took a breath as she spoke. "It has these big double doors up front, and I want to have a reception area and check-in right when you walk in. Then I would have a salon downstairs, and upstairs I would renovate the rooms to host different spa treatments."

"It doesn't sound like you're going to need to much advice from him." My dad pointed his fork in my direction. "It sounds like you've put a lot of thought into this."

"I have." She was practically beaming. "I want it to be a place that women feel welcome when they walk in and better about themselves when they leave."

"That sounds wonderful." My mom was smiling at her like she was listening to the dreams of her own child. "Then when Jim and I come to visit Liam, I could come get pampered."

"Absolutely. Maybe we could even serve some of Sarah's biscuits in the little bakery I'd love to run out of the kitchen."

My mom's eyes lit up, and I swear I could see this entire thing blowing up right before my very eyes.

...

"Mom, we're fine to take separate rooms. Brooke can sleep in the guest room and I'll take my old bedroom."

"Nonsense." She shook her head, and I tried to avoid Brooke giving me the stink eye from behind her. "You're almost thirty years old. I think it will be okay for you and your girlfriend to sleep in the same bed."

"It's not a big deal." Brooke nodded toward the closed door that held the guest bed. "I don't mind sleeping in there."

"Now hush. The both of you." My mom opened the door to my bedroom then stepped out of the way. "I put fresh sheets and blankets on his bed since his were a bit dingey. Goodnight, you two." Then she smiled and headed toward her bedroom as I ushered Brooke into my tiny ass room.

She walked around the room looking at all the shit on my walls and shelves that had been there since I was in high school as I set our bags down near the window. There were loads of football trophies from my days on the field and a few posters of half-naked girls on my walls.

If I had thought my mother was going to force us to room together, I would have asked her to shove half of this shit in the closet.

"Your parents are really nice." She ran her finger over the dust on one of my trophies.

"Yeah. They are. I think they like you a little too much though." I sat down on the corner of my bed and started pulling off my shoes.

She turned toward me, and I could feel her watching my movements. "Is that an issue? Would you rather I make them hate me?"

I tossed my shoes into the corner of the room and looked up at her. "It would be easier when this is all over." I waved my hand between the two of us, but we both knew exactly what I was talking about.

"Okay. So be a bitch from here on out." She nodded her head, but I could tell she was irritated. "Got it."

"I didn't say you had to be a bitch." I rubbed my hand down the back of my neck because I honestly wasn't sure what the hell I was saying.

"Then what exactly are you saying?" She reached for her bag and placed it on the bed beside me.

She was going through it like she was searching for gold while I answered. "I just don't want my mom to get hurt because she falls in love with you and then I rip you away."

"Don't worry." She held her clothes close to her chest as she made her way to my bedroom door. "Nobody is going to fall in love with anyone."

When the door shut behind her, I wasn't sure if she meant my mom or me, but she was right. This was nothing but a lie, and it would be over before either of us could screw up anything.

CHAPTER 7
BROOKE

I felt terrible.

I couldn't believe that I allowed Liam to talk me into this. His parents were wonderful, truly, and I felt so much guilt every time his mama smiled at me like I was somehow solely responsible for bringing all the joy into her life.

It was almost enough to make me want to kill Liam.

Because I just wanted to tell her the truth. I wanted to tell her that I wasn't dating her son, but that he was still wonderful. I was pretty sure she already knew that though.

I had spent the night with his skin plastered against mine as he curved around my body in his small bed. I could smell him all around me. Hell, the entire room smelled like him, and I wasn't naïve enough to think that it didn't affect me. That being here with him and his family wasn't going to mess with me.

But it didn't matter.

Liam Gentry was the key to making my dreams come true. I hated it. I hated that I needed him or his help, and I hated that I so willingly jumped at the opportunity.

I shifted in my seat as we pulled up to the small parking lot that was overflowing with trucks, boat trailers, and more guys in backward hats than I had ever seen.

Liam looked almost identical to the rest of them. He was wearing a plain white t-shirt, a pair of solid black swimming trunks, and a black ball cap that was thrown backward and keeping his hair out of his face, but he stood out without even trying.

It was a blessing for him, but starting to become a curse for me. Because as soon as we stepped out of his truck, every head turned in our direction, and I'm not just talking about the good ol' boys that he went to high school with. Every single female whipped their head around so quickly, it was as if the prodigal son had returned and their available bachelor meter was going haywire. And God, I didn't blame them.

There was something about him that made your baby maker wake the hell up and take notice.

I was shifting my bag on my shoulder, irrationally nervous for no good reason, and I hated that he made me this way. I never got nervous. Not for some guy and definitely not to meet his friends.

We walked up to a small dock where most of his friends were waiting, and I smiled when Ryan was the first person I saw. He didn't waste any time as he made his way over to us, and I was surprised when he wrapped his arms around me and picked me up in a hug.

He didn't have a shirt on, and his very firm, very attractive chest was buried against my hands as he squeezed me. "Well, hell." He grinned as he set me back down on my feet next to a very stiff Liam. "I didn't realize you were coming or I would have worn something nicer." He winked, and I swear I couldn't help but laugh.

"Ryan." His name sounded so rough coming out of Liam's mouth. "Don't flirt with my girlfriend in front of me or I'll throw you off the damn boat."

It was what he should have said. Any good boyfriend would have, but the way he said it with his shoulders tense and his face scrunched up like he hated the way the words tasted on his lips, made me smile.

Liam was so far out of his element.

Ladies' man or not, he had no idea what he was doing.

"Girlfriend?" Ryan raised his eyebrows like this was the news of the century, and I guess for Liam, it was.

I shrugged my shoulders, and that only seemed to piss Liam off more.

"He somehow won me over with all that charm." I waved toward his still irritated face. "I mean, how could I resist."

Ryan laughed, but Liam's eyes narrowed in my direction. "I don't know." He reached for my bag before tossing it on one of the boats. "But when you've had enough of him, you know where I'm at."

"Who is this?" one of the guys from the group asked which only seemed to catch everyone's attention. He was big, huge really, and I was pretty sure he could bench press me with one of his pinkies.

Liam seemed to snap out of his angry haze that was still pointed in Ryan's direction, and he grinned as the big man clapped his hand then patted him on the back.

Liam settled next to me again, this time gripping my hand in his. "This is Brooke, my girlfriend."

I watched as almost every female on that damn dock seemed to deflate in front of me with that one damn word. Even the ones who were clearly attached to the guy at their side.

"Brooke, this is Andy." He nodded in the big guy's direction.

"Nice to meet you, darlin'. My condolences on having to spend time with this one."

"Yeah, yeah." Liam shoved his shoulder, and I winced. I was pretty sure Andy could throw Liam halfway across this lake if he wanted to. "We heading out there or what?"

"Let's go." Andy smiled before jumping off the dock onto one of the nicest boats I had ever seen.

Liam led me toward the boat Ryan was already on.

"Where exactly are we going?" I watched as the boats took off.

"We have a spot we all meet up and tie our boats off to one another. We've been going there since high school."

Liam climbed in the boat, and when I started to step in myself, he reached up, gripping my hips in his hands, and lifted me down into the boat.

His hands felt too hot even through my clothing, and his body felt too close. "Thanks." I tucked a piece of hair behind my ear before pulling my sunglasses down over my eyes.

"No problem." He watched me for a moment before he moved toward the back of the boat and unhooked a rope as Ryan started the loud engine.

I took a seat exactly where I was, at the front of the boat, and I looked out over the water to avoid looking at Liam or Ryan.

This wasn't exactly my jam.

I didn't really do outdoors too much, and honestly, I would rather have been in the air conditioning than the sun. But I would be lying if I said it wasn't beautiful out here.

It was. Incredibly so. There were trees everywhere you looked, and steep mountainsides in the background. The water was green but as smooth as glass, and even though I really didn't have any plans on getting in it, it did look refreshing.

The sharp wind from the speed of the boat had my hair whipping around my face, and I swear ninety percent of my lip gloss was now attached to the blond strands.

By the time we finally slowed down, I was shocked by how many boats were tied together in what looked to be the deepest damn part of the lake. Yeah, there was no way in hell I would be jumping in there.

Ryan pulled the boat up next to Andy's and the guys made quick work of dropping anchor and tying us off to the other boat. There were tons of people floating in the middle of the lake, with beers in hand, and giant smiles on their faces.

One of the boats a few down from us was blaring some country music through their speakers and people were easily moving from boat to boat to talk to one another.

"You getting in?" Ryan asked as he moved to the front of the boat to tie another rope.

I looked over the edge at the endless abyss of green. "I'm not sure."

"She's getting in," Liam said from behind me, but he was fucking crazy. One, he didn't speak for me, and two, he was out of his damn mind if he thought I was getting in that water.

I looked over my shoulder just in time to catch him pulling his t-shirt over his head, and I swear to God, just one damn look at his torso was enough to make me forget that I was irritated with him only a moment ago.

He had some sort of hot guy voodoo or something.

He pulled a hot pink float that had two round seats

connected to one another from the back of the boat. I was too busy watching him that I barely noticed as Ryan jumped off the front of the boat like he wasn't worried about alligators or fish or God only knows what.

But once he was gone, I was completely aware that only Liam and I remained.

"Why didn't Jase and Sophie come again?" I picked up my bag and opened it like I was going to find something inside to save me.

"They couldn't get out of work. That's the sucky part of having a nine to five, I guess."

I picked up my phone out of my bag. "Oh. I think Kennedy called. I better call her back."

Liam pulled my phone from my hand before tossing it back down in my bag. "You're not getting out of this, Brooke. Get your ass out of those clothes and let's go."

He sat down directly across from me, as if he was waiting for a show, and I hated that I somewhat felt self-conscious in front of him. I didn't do self-conscious.

Not anymore.

I pulled my shirt over my head before tossing it in my bag, and I could feel Liam watching my every movement. I was wearing a red strapless bikini. It was modest to some, bordering on obscene to others. But I didn't care.

I pulled my shorts down my legs then faced Liam with my arms crossed. "I really don't think me getting in that lake is a good idea. I can't even touch here."

His gaze was lazy as he drug it from the tip of my toes all the way up until it reached my eyes. "Are you scared of the water?"

"No." I pointed out toward the lake where everyone else

was swimming without a damn worry. "But I can't see through this water and something could eat me."

He grinned, a huge, annoying grin. "There's nothing in this water that will eat you."

He stood up and I watched as he put the float in the water right in the front of the boat.

"Alligators." He was crazy if he thought an alligator wouldn't eat me.

"There are no alligators in Tennessee."

Hmmm, I wasn't sure if he was being honest or not. "Fish?"

"They might nibble on you, but they're not going to eat you." He grabbed a small cooler and set it in the center of the float.

That sounded terrifying.

"I didn't think you were scared of anything." He turned back toward me and tugged on my ponytail. "Get your ass on that float or I'll throw you in."

I turned my face to look at him in shock, but it was a mistake. His face was so damn close to mine, his lips barely a whisper away. It was probably the heat that was causing me not to think clearly, because all I could think about was pressing my lips against his.

"Liam, are you and your girl coming or what?" someone yelled from the water, and I was thankful for the distraction from his lips.

"Yeah." He cleared his throat, and I wondered if he was just as distracted as I was. "We're coming."

He jumped in the lake, splashing cool water onto the boat, and as soon as he came up, he patted the seat of the float. "Let's go, babe."

I walked to the edge of the boat, and I looked out. I could

see half the people watching us, and the other half pretending that they weren't. I didn't want to embarrass him in front of his friends, but wasn't he the one who said they all shouldn't like me so much.

I pressed a toe against the float, and it seemed pretty wobbly.

"Just get on the damn float, Brooke. I've never known you to be a chickenshit."

I narrowed my eyes at him behind my sunglasses. I hated that he knew how to push my buttons, but I refused to let him win. I bent down, pulling the float closer to me, and I climbed on while silently praying I didn't fall in.

My butt touched the cold water along with my feet, but miraculously everything else stayed on the float.

"Was that so hard?" Liam flicked some water at me, but I ignored him and leaned my head back into the sun. If I was going to be out here, the least I could do was get a good tan out of it.

The float started moving, hard, and I gripped the nonexistent handles while Liam started climbing onto the float with no care if it tipped over or not.

"I swear to God, Liam, if you tip this over."

He plopped into the seat without an ounce of grace and looked over at me with a smile on his face and water trickling down his neck. "What? What will you do?"

"Something." I pointed my finger at him, but he only laughed.

He wasn't scared of me in the least.

He started paddling, moving us away from our boat, and I laid back, not helping him at all.

There were at least ten other boats tied up alongside ours and probably forty people swimming and hanging out on the boats. It was odd. I had never been to a floating party like this in my life.

Several people yelled their hellos and welcome homes to Liam, and I wasn't surprised to see how many of them were vying for his attention.

"So, Brooke. What do you do?" one girl who was sitting on the edge of a boat with her feet splashing in and out of the water asked. I had already forgotten her name.

"I run a salon. You?"

Liam was talking to some guy at his side and paying us no attention.

"I'm a bartender."

She was hot, and I was sure she made tons of tips, so I told her so.

"I bet the tips are good."

"They are." She smiled. "It's the only reason I haven't quit yet. Oh. Hey, Katie!"

She was waving at a girl on a boat that just pulled up, and I wouldn't have paid her any attention if she wasn't so pretty and the guy who was supposed to be my boyfriend didn't tense up like someone had just yelled that there was a shark in the water.

I looked over at him, but he wasn't looking at me. His gaze was bouncing back and forth between the guy he was talking to and the brunette on the boat.

She was gorgeous, in that effortless beauty sort of way. Her dark hair was tied into a bun on the top of her head, but soft curls had fallen out and framed her face. Her nose was covered in freckles from the sun and good genetics, and if Liam didn't seem so affected by her, I would admit that she was by far the prettiest girl out here.

"Hey!" Katie waved over at the group with a huge smile

on her face, but I caught the moment it faltered. The moment her eyes landed on Liam.

Whatever was going on between them or had gone on between them, it had affected them both, and it was complete bullshit that something I didn't know a thing about, had no business knowing, seemed to be affecting me too.

She seemed to catch herself and the way she was staring at Liam as some guy took a seat next to her. She looked up and shared a sweet smile with him before she finally looked at me.

She still had a smile on her face, and I had a feeling that she rarely let that smile slip. It looked too practiced and perfected, almost exactly the way Liam's was. But her eyes were pinched in the corners, and I knew she wanted to know who the hell I was as badly as I wanted to know the same about her.

She stood, jerking her gaze away from me as if she couldn't take another second of it, and I watched as she jumped into the water without a second of fear.

Whoever this girl was, she had meant something to Liam or she still did, and I couldn't stop watching him as he watched her.

CHAPTER 8
LIAM

If I had known that Katie was going to be here, I would have never brought Brooke. Hell, I wouldn't have come at all.

I hadn't seen her in so long I was a little shocked looking at her. She looked almost exactly the same as the day I left, but she looked so different as well.

So much had changed.

We had both changed.

When Tucker and I decided to move away from Tennessee, I had thought Katie would be coming with us. She went everywhere with me. She had for years. While my focus was completely on her, I was a fool for not seeing that hers was on someone else. The same someone else that was now helping her back into his boat.

"Who's that?" Brooke's voice startled me, and I realized I had barely taken my eyes off Katie since she arrived.

Shit.

"That's no one." I took a long pull from my beer and tried to settle the small ache that still echoed in my chest.

"It's definitely someone." She said the words for only me to hear, and I wondered if I was crazy for thinking there was a bit of jealousy in her voice.

"Liam, it's been a while, man." I looked up at Brad as he pulled Katie into his side and wrapped an arm around her.

"It has." I nodded my head. "I've been busy."

"You here for the wedding?"

Fuck, I forgot that douchebag was friends with my cousin. I prayed him and Katie weren't going to be there. Sitting through another boring damn wedding was bad enough.

"Yeah. My mom would have killed me if I didn't come."

"How is your mom?" My gaze finally met Katie's as those words passed her lips. She didn't get to ask me that. She didn't get to pretend like she cared.

"She's good." I nodded just as Brooke's hand slid into mine.

I looked over at her, a little startled by the gesture, but I could see it in her eyes. She knew. She didn't have a clue who this girl was, but she knew that I was somehow bothered by her.

"Katie, this is my girlfriend, Brooke." I didn't take my eyes off her. "Brooke, this is Katie and Brad."

Brooke turned away from me and lifted her hand over her eyes to block the sun as she looked up at them. That one simple move did amazing things for her breasts, and if I didn't know any better, I would say she knew that too. Not that her damn breasts needed any help. I knew from the moment she pulled off her clothes and revealed that tiny red bikini beneath, I was in trouble.

"It's so nice to meet you both. I love your suit." She motioned toward Katie's frilly white bikini.

It wasn't lost on me how different the two of them were.

Katie was soft and meek, and Brooke was so far from the two of those things that I couldn't even fathom describing her in that way. She was hardheaded and in your face and completely unapologetic about who she was.

Katie looked so pretty, she had always been so beautiful, and her pretty white swimsuit only seemed to reiterate that fact. Brooke, on the other hand, wasn't pretty. That seemed like far too delicate of a word to describe her. She was fire. So damn hot, and impossible not to watch.

She was beautiful in an unforgettable sort of way. It wasn't just her looks or her perfect damn body. It was the way she was always laughing or how she made everyone around her smile. Even on the shittiest of days. When I looked at her, I felt a bit frantic because I knew I would never see beauty like this again. She was terrifying and exhilarating at the exact same time.

Because I knew getting my heart broken by a girl like Brooke would be nothing like what happened with Katie. Brooke would destroy me piece by piece, and I wasn't willing to give her the chance to do so.

I wasn't a complete and total idiot.

"Thanks." Katie was watching Brooke closely. "You too."

I grinned because I knew it was a lie. I knew Katie enough to know that she fucking hated Brooke's suit, and not because she didn't like the color or the cut. She hated it because Brooke looked so damn effortlessly beautiful in nothing but a scrap of red fabric and Katie was threatened.

Katie was always threatened.

Right on cue, she turned toward Brad, eager to kiss the guy who did nothing but drink beer with his boys and watch football ninety percent of his life, and she kissed him like she hadn't seen him in forever.

I rolled my eyes at the effort.

It wasn't fucking needed.

It didn't bother me. It seemed to bother Brooke though.

She squeezed my hand, bringing my attention back to her, and honestly, I'm not sure how I ever looked away.

"She the ex?" She gently nodded her head toward Brad's boat.

"That's the one." I was staring at her lips as she licked them.

"No wonder you're scared of relationships. She looks like she's probably as good at fucking as she is at making you jealous." She ran her hand up my chest and I laughed as I watched the movement as if she was a viper about to strike at any moment. "Which is not at all, right?"

"Right." I nodded my head, but I could barely register what she was saying with the way her nails bit into my skin.

"Then don't let it show, lover boy." Her fingers reached my chin and she tilted it in her direction as she moved her face closer to mine.

I knew this was fake.

Everything about it was.

But the way she watched my mouth didn't seem fake, the way her breath caught as her lips pressed against mine. She nibbled on my bottom lip, and everything was suddenly too real.

I ran my tongue against her mouth, and she let out the tiniest moan as she let me inside. The way she tasted didn't seem fake. Neither did the way her hand wrapped around the back of my neck or the way her tongue was fighting with mine for more.

A loud whistle rang out and I barely registered it. It wasn't until I heard Andy's loud mouth say, "Well, ladies. Pack it up. It seems our golden boy, Liam, has finally found the one," that some sense was finally knocked into me.

I pulled my mouth away from Brooke with a laugh, and I avoided her eyes as I smiled.

I may have been their golden boy, but I hadn't found anything. I was going to keep telling myself that over and over until I finally believed it.

CHAPTER 9
BROOKE

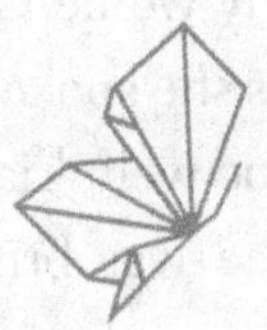

"Go to Tennessee with Liam," they said. "It will be a good vacation."

Vacation my ass.

Unless you considered getting whiplash from the resident golden boy a vacation. Which let me be clear, I didn't.

I had just gotten done telling Kennedy that too. She wanted to know all about it.

Was I having fun?

Were we in love yet?

That girl, she had jokes.

No. I was not having fun. Okay. Technically, I was having a little bit of fun, but I didn't know one moment from the next if Liam was going to be hot or cold.

It was confusing, and it was fucking with my head.

"Good morning." Liam's mom, Sarah, was sitting on her front porch when I walked outside. I had no idea where Liam was. I just knew he wasn't in the bed when I woke up and that he had been acting weird ever since I kissed him yesterday.

"Morning." I took a seat in the rocking chair beside her.

"Liam went to the store with his dad to get some things to fix that old fence." She lifted her coffee cup in the direction of a fence that looked perfectly fine to me.

"Okay." I pulled one of my knees to my chest and slowly rocked in the chair.

"Liam doesn't let many women in, you know." She had a gentle smile on her face as she spoke.

"I know." I knew all too well. Liam didn't let anyone in.

"When he told me he was bringing you home for the wedding, I just about fell out of my chair." She laughed and looked out over the view of the mountains in the distance. "The last girl I saw him with just about broke his heart. Or maybe she actually did."

"Katie." I finally said her name out loud. She had been all I had been able to think about since yesterday. The way she looked at Liam, but more importantly, the way Liam looked at her.

"Yeah. He tell you about her?"

"Not really." I was honest with the woman for once. "But we saw her yesterday, and I saw the way he looked at her."

She nodded as if she understood without even having to experience it. "She was his high school sweetheart. It didn't matter how much I begged him to slow down, he thought that girl was going to be his future."

Her words were like a sharp knife to the chest.

"But I knew she wasn't. She never looked at him the way he looked at her. She was always too busy looking somewhere else." She turned her head and looked at me. "Not you though. You look at him like he hung the moon and all the stars."

I was a little stunned by her words. I looked at him like that? I wasn't meaning to.

"Don't look so shocked." She chuckled, and I tried to school my face. "My boy looks at you the same way."

"He doesn't." I shook my head. I could pretend to be his girlfriend, but the last thing I wanted was for her to think her son was madly in love with me when it was the furthest thing from the truth.

"He does, love. It doesn't matter what that boy tries to hide. I'm his mama, and I know I've never seen my boy look at someone the way he looks at you."

Yeah, because he was a damn good actor.

"What happened with Katie?"

She leaned her head back, and I had a feeling she hated reliving this story. She hated remembering how her son got hurt.

"He was in love with her. They had been dating since they were sixteen years old. He couldn't see a future that didn't involve her."

Stab. Stab. Stab.

"When he decided to start a business with Tucker, he thought she would be with him. But then he found out that she was sleeping with Brad." She shook her head. "I never liked that boy, and God knows he doesn't hold a candle to my son."

Hear, hear.

"She begged Liam to take her back. Right here on this porch." She pointed down at the wood deck. "She was a blubbering mess and kept saying it was a mistake, but he didn't budge. Thank God. Once he found out that she cheated on him, he was done. Then he ran out of town with Tucker as fast as he could go."

I shook my head, trying to imagine a heartbroken Liam. I didn't even like the thought. "I didn't know."

"I'm not surprised." She gave me a weak smile. "That's one thing about Liam. He's always kept everything to himself."

"Yeah." I completely understood that. "He's a hard one to crack."

"He'll crack for you though. I just know it." She seemed so sure of herself, and I hated that she was so wrong. Not only because I didn't want this whole thing to blow up and hurt her, but I was worried it would hurt me too.

We were both silent for a moment. I had no idea what she was thinking about, but all I could do is imagine how this all would end.

"Here he is now." Sarah pointed to the truck pulling into the driveway, and even though I knew it shouldn't, my stomach tensed as I watched him climb out of the passenger seat.

"Hey there, sleepyhead." He picked up a piece of my hair before letting it fall against my shoulder.

"Hey."

I didn't know how to deal with this Liam. Sure, he was physically the same guy standing in front of me, but he had never been like this at home. He was always so standoffish, so cold almost.

"I almost have him talked into it, Sarah." His dad was climbing up the front porch steps with a small bag in his hands.

"No. He doesn't," Liam responded quickly. Too quickly.

"Talked into what?" I was hella curious now.

"Dad's trying to talk me into playing in some flag football game tonight, but I'm not doing it."

"It's not just some game." His dad huffed. "It's our Masonville High alumni football team, and we're playing our rival tonight. We could really use Liam's arm."

"It's a bunch of old men reliving their glory days."

"Not true," Sarah said from beside me. "There are several younger guys on the team now. Brad even starts for Valley."

I watched her as she said the words, and I swear she knew what she was doing. She knew the exact thing that would make Liam react.

"Yeah." His dad nodded his head. "And he's still good too. Valley High will beat us for sure tonight if he shows up."

I snorted, and all three heads turned in my direction.

"Oh, sorry." I held my hand over my mouth, but I couldn't stop laughing.

"What's so funny?" Liam cocked his head.

"Masonville High and Valley High. Arch-rivals. We really are in the south, aren't we?" I raised an eyebrow at him. I felt like I was suddenly in the middle of some country soap opera.

"Are you making fun of us?" Liam moved in my direction, but I held my hands up to block him.

"No." I giggled again. "I just never thought I'd hear a conversation like this in real life."

"Dad, add me to the roster." He bent down in front of me as his dad did an adorable little fist pump into the air. "I need to go deal with this one before the game."

I rolled my eyes. Liam wouldn't know how to deal with me if he tried. Especially not in front of his parents.

He wrapped his hands around my hips, and I tightened my hands on the arms of the rocking chair. "You wouldn't dare."

But there was a spark of playfulness in his eyes that I had never seen before. Definitely not directed at me, and I had a feeling that he would dare.

He lifted me up like I didn't weigh a thing, and I shrieked as his shoulder knocked into my stomach.

His mom and dad were standing right there, and this barbarian threw me over his shoulder like I was his property.

"Liam, put me down!"

His dad chuckled, and I swear I saw his mama wink at him as he moved away from them.

I bounced on his shoulder as he carried me up the stairs. "Liam." I hesitated, trying to come up with his middle name, but realized that I didn't know it. "Wait, what's your middle name?"

"Not important." He was still walking, and for a moment, I wondered where the hell he was taking me.

"I bet it's something super country like Jethro or Billy Bob." I giggled just as he tossed me down on his bed.

"My middle name is not Billy Bob." He rolled his eyes, but I was more concerned about the way his thighs were touching the edges of mine.

"Jethro was my first guess."

He moved into my space, his face coming close to mine, and I tried to catch my breath from being thrown over his shoulder and being thrown into another situation where the only thing I wanted to do was press my lips against his.

"Do you have a problem with country boys?" He wrapped his fingers around my wrist, tugging me closer to him.

"No problem." I blew some hair out of my face. "I've just never experienced one out in the wild like this."

"You literally see me all the time."

"Yeah, but you're not quite this country at home. Being in the south really brings the redneck out in you."

"I'm not a redneck." He lifted the same piece of hair I was struggling with only a moment before and tucked it behind my ear. "There's a difference between a country boy and a redneck."

"And what if I don't like country boys?" He was so close to me now I could practically taste the scent of him on my tongue.

"You don't really have a choice. You're dating one." He raised an eyebrow in challenge.

"Fake dating one." I pointed out the obvious. A point that neither one of us were in any danger of forgetting.

"Semantics."

He looked down at my mouth, and I wondered if he was questioning the semantics of this arrangement as hard as I was. But Liam wasn't as easily swayed as me. He pushed away from the bed, and I took a deep breath as I watched him walk toward his small closet.

"You have a really nice ass. Did you know that? As your fake girlfriend, it would be wrong for me not to point that out."

I was thinking about how easily I could get used to this view just as something hit me directly in the face.

I picked up the shirt just as he said, "Go get gussied up. We have a game to win tonight."

"Why do I have to get gussied up for your grown man football game?"

"Because, darlin'." He put an extra strong drawl on the pet name and I swear my stomach tightened instantly. "This might be fake, but I'm still going to reap the benefits. And as your fake boyfriend, your ass is much better than nice and tonight you're going to be my personal cheerleader."

I held up the jersey with Gentry on the back.

"Do I get pom-poms?"

He grabbed a pair of gym shorts and boxers before making his way to the door. "As long as you're shaking your ass and chanting my name, I'll get you whatever you want."

CHAPTER 10
BROOKE

I took what Liam said to heart, and I was dying at the way his mama kept smiling as she looked at me.

Him and his dad left the house two hours ago to go get warmed up which Sarah told me meant drink some beers before the game. The game was happening on the high school football field, and I was surprised by how many people filled the stadium as Liam's mama and I walked up.

"I know I'm his mom, and I probably shouldn't say this, but Liam's going to die when he sees you."

I hoped she wasn't wrong. I put in a lot of work for this cheerleader job of mine.

I put on his jersey, but it practically swallowed me whole. So I rolled up the sleeves and tied up the back to pull it taut against my chest and stomach. The tiniest sliver of my stomach was showing just above the smallest pair of blue jean shorts I owned.

I questioned not wearing any of it, especially knowing his mom and dad would be here, but Liam was the one who told me he wanted them to like me less. Plus, Sarah's reaction was basically a squeal of delight when she saw me.

I'm pretty positive it's because she secretly wants me to get pregnant.

I don't know how big of a secret that is to Liam, but we spent a good majority of the ride here talking about whether or not I wanted babies while I simultaneously freaked out.

I wasn't ready to have babies.

I didn't even have a real boyfriend, for crying out loud. Not that I could tell her that.

We took a seat in the front row, and I took a second to look around me at all the people I didn't know.

I spotted Katie sitting with a group of other girls, and she was dressed completely normal. She had on a pair of jeans with a white tank top and her brown hair laid against her shoulders in a pile of curls.

Suddenly, I felt foolish.

It was insane that I was allowing this girl who I didn't even know to have this power over me. But Liam had loved her once upon a time, and I had never even come close.

But here I was in his old football jersey with some eye black under my eyes looking like some sort of lovesick fool.

I was staring at Katie and her friends so hard I barely noticed Sophie as she ran in my direction and pulled me into a hug.

"You're here!"

"I'm here." I laughed.

"Hey, Jase." He was standing behind her looking as beautiful as always.

"Brooke." He nodded toward me with a smirk, and I knew that he probably knew exactly why I was here. "Mrs. G."

Sophie let me go and held me at arm's length as she looked me up and down. "You look so damn hot."

"It's too much." I looked down at my outfit.

"No." She shook her head. "It's perfect." She looked over at Sarah and gave her a small wave. "Come to the concession stand with me."

"I'll be right back," I said to Sarah, but Sophie was already pulling me away.

As soon as we made it out of earshot, she started in on me. "I talked to Kennedy. She told me what you're doing."

"Oh. She told you I was out here looking like a fool for my fake boyfriend." I waved down at my outfit.

"Are you two fucking?" She cocked her head to the side.

"No. We're not fucking," I whisper-yelled because Sophie was being incredibly loud.

"Well, you're going to be once he sees you in this outfit. I kind of want to fuck you myself."

I rolled my eyes but couldn't help grinning. "You're ridiculous."

"No. I'm honest." We got in line for the concession stand, but she kept up with the questions. "Have y'all at least kissed?"

"Yes. Of course."

"And?" She waved her hand, asking for more details.

"And what?"

"How the hell was it? I bet Liam's a good kisser."

I nodded my head. "He is."

"Did you get little butterflies in your stomach when you kissed?" She was far too excited about the prospect.

"No." I looked at her like she was crazy even though she was far too on point. "I'm too damn old for butterflies, plus we're fake dating, remember?"

"That doesn't make his tongue fake."

"No. It sure doesn't."

"See." She snapped her fingers. "I knew he was a good kisser."

While she was right about his kissing skills, I couldn't stop thinking about the time he used his tongue a little farther south. Heat spread across my chest, and for a second I wondered what the hell was happening to me. I didn't blush, and I sure as hell didn't fall for a guy simply because he was good at going down on me.

Okay, to be fair, he was far better than good.

Life-altering, even.

But there were plenty guys out there that could rock my world.

"Being a good kisser isn't going to make me fall for the guy. This is a simple business deal."

"Uh huh." She looked like she believed me about as much as I did. "You keep telling yourself that."

"Oh, wow. Sophie Moore, is that you?"

As soon as I heard Katie's voice, my heart fell into my stomach. She was standing behind us in line, only one other person between us, and prayed harder than I had ever prayed before that she didn't just overhear our conversation.

And of course the main reason was because I didn't want her to tell Liam's parents and ruin this entire rouse we had going, but more than that, I couldn't stand the thought of her thinking Liam had to make a business deal to get a girl to come home with him.

To be happy.

It didn't matter if that was the truth of what happened.

The bigger truth was that I would have come anyway for him.

"Katie, how are you?" Sophie moved to hug her, and the guy behind us seemed annoyed so I offered for him to go in front of us.

Because being closer to Katie was exactly where I wanted to be.

"I'm good." She smiled, and I swear her smile was big and natural and real, but I still hated it. "Just about to watch Brad kick some Masonville butt tonight."

I wanted to roll my eyes. The girl didn't even say ass and that annoyed me far more than it should have.

"Good luck with that. Liam's playing tonight, and he brought his good luck charm with him." They both looked up at me, and I swear the look on Sophie's face told me exactly how much she was enjoying this.

"Oh, right. Brooke, right?"

"Right." I nodded my head. She knew my name.

"How long have you and Liam been together?" She seemed genuinely curious.

"A couple months," I recited the answer we had practiced even though I wanted nothing more than to tell her we had been madly in love for years.

"Officially." Sophie rolled her eyes playfully. "These two have been dancing around each other like two lovesick puppies since the day they met though. I've never seen him so smitten."

Katie physically flinched. Only slightly, but I noticed. And for the first time since I met her, I actually felt a little sorry for her.

"I don't know about that."

"No. She's right." I was so surprised by Katie's words that I just stared at her. "I don't think I've ever seen him this happy."

"He makes me really happy." Those words slipped off my tongue far too easily. "He makes it easy."

"He does." She nodded, and even though she looked regretful and only a moment before I felt sorry for her, I wanted to knock her head off her shoulders in that moment.

I wanted to scream at her.

If he made it so easy, then why did you hurt him? Why did you fuck over the best fucking guy for that douchebag you are now dating?

I didn't say any of that though. Instead, I turned toward the concession stand and ordered far too much food for Liam's mom and I and a couple extra waters for Liam and his dad.

Sophie and Katie were still chatting a bit, about people I had no clue who they were, but all I could think about was Liam.

It was all I ever seemed to think about anymore.

"Well, we're going to head out there. The game should be starting any minute now," Sophie said as she piled her own food into her arms.

"Okay. I'll catch y'all later." We started to walk off, but Katie called out to us again. "Jeremy is having a bonfire tonight after the game to celebrate. Both teams are welcome of course."

I had no idea who the hell Jeremy was, but that didn't sound exactly awful.

"Thanks! We'll let the guys know."

Sophie was watching me as we walked away. "What, Soph?"

"You know who that was, right?"

"I do." I nodded my head. "Liam told me she was his ex, but his mom told me the details."

"I hate her."

I was shocked because she just seemed so friendly with her.

She could see the shock on my face too. "What? I'm not in high school anymore. I've already decked her once for her mistake. We don't need to hash it out again."

"Wait." I almost dropped my food as I swiveled in her direction. "You punched her?"

"Yup." She looked so damn proud. "Tucker and Liam wouldn't let me say shit to her after what she did to Liam, so I waited until the day they left. Poor girl was traumatized, but it felt so damn good. She deserved it."

We kept walking back to our seats. "I didn't think I could love you more, but I do."

She laughed, and I was so distracted by her that I almost missed Liam leaning against the fence in front of Jase and his mom. He was wearing a pair of gym shorts that hung low on his hips and showed off every single ridge of his impressive stomach.

He was so incredibly handsome, and I swear every female within a hundred-foot radius had their eyes on him but he was looking at me.

I handed his mom her food and set my food down next to her as I took a moment to avoid him and the way he was looking at me like he wanted to eat me alive. I turned back toward him, two water bottles in my hands, and I held them out to him. "I got you and your dad a water."

I was pretty sure he hadn't registered a word I said. He reached out for my hand, tugging me toward him, and my chest pressed against his.

He stared down at me without saying a word, and I could barely breathe. This was where everything became so confusing. This right here. It felt real. Far too real. But I didn't know where the truth began and the lies ended.

Was this for him or was this for everyone else?

"What?" My voice sounded as breathless as I felt.

"You really took the cheerleader thing to heart, huh?" His hand moved to my hip. It was an innocent touch, but I felt like he was stripping me bare right here for everyone to see.

"I'm nothing if not a little extra." I shrugged as he grinned.

"Are you going to cheer for me?" He moved his face closer to mine and pressed a kiss on my jaw that was so gentle I almost thought I imagined it.

"If that's what you want."

His lips were now right against my ear. "I want a lot of things."

I swear to God a chill ran through my body and everyone in those bleachers or on that field had a front-row view of Liam turning me to putty in his hands.

"If we lose this game, I'm blaming you."

"Me?" I turned my face to look at him, but that only put his mouth incredibly close to mine. "What did I do?"

"You came here looking like a wet fucking dream, and I'm going to be distracted." His hand tightened on my hip, and I swear if we weren't in front of his whole damn town I would say fuck this agreement. I wanted Liam, and despite our history, I knew he wanted me too.

I just didn't know how far that want went.

But we were in front of an audience and that audience included people who were supposed to believe we were in love.

"Don't blame your lack of football skills on my outfit."

"Alright." He chuckled and finally faced me again. "I'll win this game just for you."

"Don't write checks your ass can't cash, Golden Boy." As soon as the words left my lips, his mouth was on mine. The kiss was passionate or soul-searing, but it was sudden and unplanned and real.

And I couldn't do anything but stare after him as he took the waters from my hands and headed out onto the field.

I took a seat between his mom and Sophie and nudged Sophie in the side to get her to stop smirking like a loon.

She leaned toward me, whispering where only I could hear. "You're right. Like looked super official. No funny business at all."

I was so screwed.

She knew it. I knew it, but I couldn't let Liam know it.

It was the last thing I needed.

This was a fake relationship, and I didn't want my soon-to-be business partner realizing that I was making really poor business decisions from the get-go.

Especially when it came to him.

They took the field, and I smiled as I looked out at Liam's dad standing near him on the field. I didn't have a clue what position he was playing. In all honesty, the only one I actually knew was that Liam was the quarterback.

"Let's go boys!" Sarah yelled from beside me just as the ball hit Liam's hands.

I wasn't at all surprised at how good he was. He threw the ball, it landed in the hands of the other player perfectly, and before I even knew what was happening, they were scoring.

I jumped to my feet, cheering with Liam's mom, and we high-fived just as the other offense took the field.

The game went back and forth for a long time. The score was practically even the whole game, but then Liam got into a rhythm and the other team didn't stand a chance.

It was the fourth quarter, thank God. It was hot as hell out here and this jersey wasn't nearly as breathable as it looked. Liam looked like he was having a blast, and I loved seeing him so carefree and happy.

He caught the snap, Sarah told me that was what they called it, and cocked his arm back to throw the ball. He didn't even see the guy coming at him from the side.

None of us did.

They were playing flag football, but this guy hit Liam like he was trying to kill him.

Liam hit the ground and I jumped out of my seat. I leaned against the railing as I watched him grab his left shoulder. He was hurt. You could see it all over his face, and my stomach was in my throat as I watched him.

His dad was by his side and his mom by mine, and everyone seemed to be silent as we watched his dad grip his opposite hand and lift him to his feet.

Everyone was clapping as he walked off the field, but not me. I was ready to kill that asshole that hit him.

"Why would he do that?" I had no idea who I was asking. I was already walking down to the opposite end of the field, and I was going to give that guy a piece of my mind.

But then I looked down at the field and saw Liam jogging beside me.

"Where you going, babe?"

I pointed to the other team. "I'm going to knock some sense into that jerk."

He laughed and that only seemed to piss me off more. "Calm down. I'm okay."

I stopped in my tracks and looked at him. He was still holding his shoulder and his arm was bent against his chest. He didn't look okay to me.

"He hurt you."

He was smiling, but I didn't know what the hell he had to smile about. "It's all right. I'm fine."

The game was still going on behind him, but as I looked around, it seemed everyone was watching us instead of the game.

"I was going to kick his ass." I crossed my arms which only made him grin bigger.

"I could see that."

I didn't see it as amusing as he did. "Are you hurt?"

"I'm sore." He was still staring at me. "As long as you can help me get dressed, I'll be fine."

I rolled my eyes, but I couldn't help but smile. "I can do that."

He stepped closer to me, and even though he was covered in sweat and a bit of dirt, I wasn't sure he had ever looked hotter than in that moment.

"You really pulled off the part of the worried girlfriend." He was teasing me, and I rolled my eyes.

"I didn't want them to think I didn't care when I just sat there." I shrugged my shoulders, but he knew I cared.

"Uh huh."

"Weren't you supposed to be winning this game for me or something?"

He looked toward the game that was winding down then back at me. "Did you happen to look at the scoreboard?"

"I did." I pointed out to the field. "But right now I see your dad in that end zone thing with the ball. So it looks like he's winning the game."

"Motherfucker." He pointed his good hand at me. "You're still my cheerleader."

"Of course I am."

He walked back to where his team was celebrating. "Don't forget it either."

CHAPTER 11
LIAM

We were back at my parents' house, and I wasn't sure I had ever been babied so much in my entire life. Between my mom and Brooke, you would have thought I had a concussion instead of a banged-up shoulder.

Don't get me wrong. It hurt like a bitch, but it wasn't something that I couldn't handle.

But the attention was still nice. Especially from Brooke.

I wasn't sure I had ever seen her pay so much attention to anyone other than Kennedy. If I had known getting a little bit banged up was the trick to it, I would have done this the day we got here.

"I'm fine." I pulled her down onto my lap instead of letting her check the bruising on my shoulder for the hundredth time.

She rolled her eyes, but she still wrapped an arm around my good shoulder. "I have to admit. I don't know much about sports injuries, but I think you're too old for this."

I poked her in the side, and she let out a little yelp. "I'm not too old for anything." It was a complete lie. I was definitely too old for this. "That asshole shouldn't have hit me like that."

"You're damn right he shouldn't have." Dad sounded as pissed as Brooke was earlier.

When I saw her marching down the line of the field, I knew the little spitfire was going to cause a scene. I should have let her give that guy a piece of her mind, but I wasn't sure I had the strength to pull her off of him with my shoulder if she went too far. And Brooke would go too far.

It was one of the things I loved about her.

She almost never held back.

Except around me, and I hated that I made her feel the need to do so.

My dad handed us both a beer, and Brooke started to stand from my lap but I held her against me. I didn't want her going anywhere.

She looked down at me, and I felt surrounded by her. Her hair was draped over her shoulder and had the slightest hint of coconut, and her body fit perfectly against mine as I held her to me. Her hip was in my hand, and my fingers were aching with the urge to lift my jersey just the tiniest bit and feel more of her skin against mine.

She took a sip of her beer and looked out over the back yard. We were sitting on my parents' deck, and the stars were so damn clear. I almost forgot what they looked like.

I hadn't seen a sky like this in a long time. Not since the last time I was home.

"Brooke, are we still good for dress shopping tomorrow?" my mom asked as she stood from the swing she and my dad had been sitting on.

"Yeah." Brooke nodded and appeared genuinely excited.

"As long as this one can take care of himself while we're gone."

"I'll be fine," I grumbled. I wasn't a damn baby.

My mom just laughed then reached out for my dad's hand. "Then we're headed to bed. We'll see you all in the morning."

My dad followed her without a second thought, and the more I thought about it, he always had. I was pretty sure he would follow her through anything.

"Goodnight, guys." Brooke ran her hand over my hair as she spoke and her body settled into mine. I wasn't sure if she had realized she had done it, but I did. I noticed everything about her.

"'Night." My parents slipped through the back door and left me and Brooke alone under the stars.

The night was quiet except for the sound of crickets and the slight breeze blew through the trees, but Brooke wasn't planning to sit back and enjoy it. As soon as my parents were gone, she went to stand, but I held her harder against me.

"Where are you going?" I leaned my head back against the chair.

"Your parents are gone." She looked to the back door as if maybe she missed them still standing there.

But she wouldn't find them. I just wasn't ready to give her up yet.

I tightened my hand on her hip and ignored what she said. "Tell me something about you that no one else knows."

She was so tense you would have thought I'd asked her to marry me. It only made me want to know her secrets more.

"What do you want to know?" She looked out to where the trees were barely lit up by the stars, and I knew she was just avoiding looking at me.

"Anything." I ran my thumb over her skin. "Tell me something about your family."

She looked back at me, and I could tell this was the last thing she wanted to talk about. I hated knowing that she was getting a front-row seat at my past, but I barely knew a thing about her.

"Tell me something about why you don't ever come home." I knew she said it because she thought it would shut me up, but she was wrong. If she wanted to play this game, we would play it.

"It's good to come back for a few days, but I just needed to get out of here."

"Because of her?" Her words were soft, and I could tell she regretted them as soon as she said them.

"Yeah." I nodded my head, and I couldn't lie and say that even talking to her about Katie made my chest feel tight. "Because of her and what everyone thought of me because of what she did. I just couldn't take it anymore."

I could tell she wanted to ask more, but her lips didn't budge. She stared down at me with sympathy in her eyes, and I fucking hated it.

"I don't know how much you know." I had no doubt that my mama or Sophie had already opened their mouths about what happened. That was one thing you could always count on in this town. "But I was completely blindsided when Katie cheated on me. I hadn't really prepared for what life would be like without her." I let out a deep breath.

I hadn't talked about Katie in so long that it felt foreign. I sure as hell didn't talk about what she had done and how it fucked me up.

"I really don't like that girl." The way she scrunched up

her nose in disgust was absolutely adorable, and I wanted to lean forward and press a small kiss there.

But I didn't.

"Me either. Not anymore."

"Is she the reason you don't date anymore?" She tucked a piece of hair behind her ear, and I knew that asking that question made her nervous.

I looked at the sky for a second, debating how to answer her. "Yeah." I decided on honesty. "She kind of fucked me up for a while. What about you?"

"What about me?" She looked down at me with hesitation, and I knew she didn't want to talk about her. It was too bad. I gave and now it was her turn.

"Why don't you date? Why did you leave home?"

"I honestly don't know." She shrugged but that was a lie. I knew it from the moment she opened her mouth. "My family isn't like yours. I haven't been back home in a really long time."

She looked like her family was the last thing she wanted to talk about, but I couldn't get over the urge to know more about her. I wanted to know everything.

"Then what are they like?"

She pulled away from me, turning her back on the outside world and facing me. "My dad left a long time ago," she hesitated. "My mom was more interested in chasing men with money than taking care of her daughter."

"I'm sorry." I didn't know why, but it was the last thing I expected her to say. Brooke was so strong and independent, and I expected her to say that she came from someone who helped make her that way.

But I guess she did.

"She didn't believe she was worth a thing without a man, and she pushed those same beliefs on me every day."

I winced and all I could think about was our current arrangement and how I must have made her feel. "You know that's not true."

She shrugged her shoulders and I could practically see her trying to block out my words.

I reached over and gently ran my thumb over her cheek. "You're nothing like her."

She stared straight ahead, and I knew nothing I was saying was getting through to her.

"Brooke, look at me." I moved closer to her and turned her face to look at me. "You are not your mother."

"I know that." Her answer was instant, but I didn't think she believed it.

I couldn't stop staring at her mouth, and as much as I didn't want her to think she ever had to rely on me for anything, an overwhelming need for her coursed through my veins.

I wanted to take her worries and destroy them all. I wanted her to need me even if that was the last thing she wanted.

Because I was starting to think I needed her.

I looked up at her, her gaze holding mine. "Tell me something else about you."

I needed her to keep talking before I did something stupid like breaking all the damn rules and kissing her for nobody else but me.

"What do you want to know?" She worked her lip between her teeth.

"I don't know."

"I'm a pretty open book." She shrugged her shoulders, but it was just another facade she put on.

"That's a lie." I leaned back in the chair and pulled her farther into my chest. "I used to think that, but you're not. You just like people to believe you are."

"What about you?" she asked defensively, and I knew that I hit a nerve. "I barely know anything about you and I'm supposed to be this smitten girlfriend."

I grinned. She was so damn cute when she got angry. "You play the smitten girlfriend pretty well."

She rolled her eyes and huffed.

So I gave her something I never told anyone. "I hated playing football."

"What?" She turned her head to look at me. She looked genuinely shocked.

"Yeah." I nodded. "I was good at it. Really damn good at it, and I liked that. But the pressure and expectations to be good at something I didn't love, it was overwhelming."

"Why didn't you just quit?"

If only it was that simple.

"Did you see how excited my dad was tonight? Imagine that times a hundred and that's how excited he was during my high school days."

"So your parents expected too much out of you and mine expected too little." She wasn't comparing. She was just stating our reality.

She laid her head on my shoulder and I could feel her breath go in and out against my neck. She seemed sad, and I hated that I brought all this up.

I hated that anyone had ever made her feel this way.

"What about Kennedy?" There was someone she loved. Someone who could make her feel better.

"What about her?"

"How did the two of you end up together?" I couldn't imagine a time when the two of them didn't have each other. They were so opposite but so in tune with each other that it was crazy.

The two of them drove me crazy most of the time, but it was easy to see how much they loved each other. They treated each other like they were the only person they had, and I guess before Tucker came around, they were.

"When I moved to Pennsylvania, I had no idea what I was doing. I just knew that I had a limited income and needed somewhere to live." She smiled like it was one of the best memories of her life. "I met Kennedy on the first day of my job when we were both waiting tables. She didn't like me, and I most certainly did not like her."

She chuckled and I could imagine the two of them completely clashing when they first met.

"What changed?"

"I don't know." She settled further against me. I was basically holding her now. "She's too damn funny not to like, and I guess I just rubbed off on her. We decided to move in together within the first week."

"The rest is history, huh?"

"Exactly."

The silence between us amplified the gentle swirl of the wind, and I tried to think of what else to ask her. There were a million things running through my head, but none of them felt like things I should be asking her. None of it felt like I had any right.

"What's your favorite color?"

She chuckled like it was the most ridiculous question, and I guess it was. "Green. You?"

"Green." I couldn't help smile at the similarity. "I honestly expected you to say pink."

"Got to keep them guessing." Her slender shoulder moved in a shrug against my chest. Her eyes were drifting closed, and I watched as her chest rose and fell at a gentle pace.

"Yeah. I guess you do."

She didn't respond. Her body was soft and molded to mine as if it was made to fit there. She looked beautiful as she slept. Her face free of her fears and the burdens she carried.

She didn't move as I ran my thumb across her jaw, and I couldn't stop myself as I shifted forward and pressed a barely-there kiss against her cheek.

The two of us were going to be working together soon, and it concerned me how happy it made me. Not because I was particularly excited about this business. Sure, I did think we could make money at it, but I was excited to be able to see her more often. To see her in her element when she wasn't stressed and bored to death from a job that was killing her.

I couldn't wait to see what she would do when the people around her didn't assume she knew nothing. When someone believed in her.

Shifting her in my arms, my shoulder screamed as I lifted her and headed for the door. I didn't give a shit how banged up my arm was, there was no way I was waking her up after she had finally opened up to me, even if just the smallest bit, then fell asleep in my arms.

The stairs creaked under my feet as I led us to my bedroom, and I bit back a groan of pain as I leaned forward and laid her on the bed. I expected her to let go of me then, to turn her back to me like she had every other night since we had been here, but she clung to me like I was a lifeline.

I settled down next to her, and I pushed her silky hair out of her face as she buried it in my chest.

I knew we probably shouldn't have been doing this. I should have moved, not pulled her in closer and took a deep breath of her scent like I may never smell her again. I should have turned my back to her and redrawn the line in the sand before either of us got confused.

But I didn't do any of those things. I pulled her closer to me, and I fell asleep while everything was still a blur.

CHAPTER 12
BROOKE

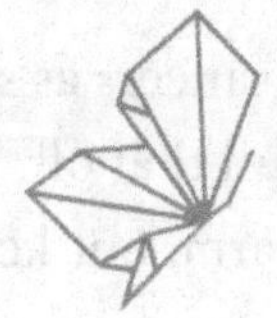

I could barely pay attention to a thing Liam's mom said.

Not when the way I woke up plastered to Liam this morning kept playing in my head like a loop. It wasn't just me either. He was holding me against him like I was meant to be there, and it felt like I was.

But I was tired and confused, and I didn't have a clue how I even got to his room in the first place. The last thing I remembered was playing twenty-one questions on the back deck while I sat in Liam's lap.

Liam's lap, where I must have fallen asleep like he was my personal bed. Oh God. He was probably so ready to get me off him that he carried me up those stairs. With a hurt shoulder that he should have been more concerned about than me.

I slipped out of his bed before he woke up, and somehow I managed to avoid him before his mom and I left the house.

I told his mom that he was probably just tired from the game the night before. I told myself that he was probably just avoiding me as much as I was avoiding him.

"What do you think of this one?" Sarah held up a pretty maroon dress that looked far too frumpy for a woman like her.

"It's pretty." I shifted through the dresses in front of me. "But this one would look amazing." I held up a silver dress that had just the slightest amount of shimmer and the perfect cut for her body.

Her eyes got as big as saucers as she looked at it.

"I don't think I can pull that off." She tucked the maroon dress in the curve of her arm, but kept looking at the dress I held up with interest.

"Just try it on." I loaded it on the pile I had for myself. "If you don't like it, we can put it back."

"You're right." She nodded and kept going through the racks. "Are you excited about the wedding?"

"Yeah," I lied. It wasn't so much that I wasn't excited about going to the wedding. The wedding would be fine. But it also meant the end of this. This charade between Liam and I would be over, and our life and our relationship would go back to normal.

I wasn't sure how to feel about that.

I didn't know how I would handle it.

Because I wouldn't be the same after this. No matter how hard I tried to keep my head on straight or my heart on lock, I knew I wasn't strong enough to withstand him.

No matter how easily he would return to normal when we got home, I would be affected.

But I was a pro at hiding my feelings, and this would be no different. I could smile at Liam at work and I could joke when he brought another girl around and pretend like I wasn't going insane with jealousy.

I knew I could.

"I'm going to be sad when you all leave." Sarah led us to the dressing room, and I closed the door to my stall as she kept talking. "Of course, I'm going to miss Liam, but I'm going to miss you too."

I hated her words.

I hated that she was so perfect and caring and made me comfortable without even trying.

I hated that we were hurting her for no good reason.

The urge to tell her the truth was on the tip of my tongue, but I could never do that to Liam. Regardless of where we ended up after this, he trusted me, and I wouldn't betray that trust even if that meant I was going to hurt his mama when this all ended.

Because she would be hurt.

She had so much false hope and dreams, and it was all our fault.

"I'll miss you too." I was being completely honest. I wouldn't tell Liam this, but I fell in love with Sarah that first moment I met her in her kitchen. She was so vastly different from my own mother, and even though I didn't actually miss my own mom, I did miss the idea of what she should have been.

Sarah was that.

She had me laughing over flour and biscuit dough, and she made it easy to fall into the role I was brought here to play.

Liam had so much of her in him. Even if he tried to hide it most of the time.

"When Jim and I come to visit Liam, maybe the two of us can plan something with just the two of us. A spa day or another shopping trip." She was in the stall next to me, and she was so sincere.

I felt like the walls were closing in around me.

"I'd love that." I sank to my ass and stared at myself in the mirror. My chest was starting to rise and fall in panic. What the fuck was I doing?

I didn't even look like myself. I hadn't put a trace of makeup on my face this morning which never happened. I never left my apartment without makeup, but somehow, I looked happier in that moment than my reflection had looked in a long time.

My skin was kissed by the sun, my blond hair piled on top of my head in a messy bun, and I felt happy.

But it was all a facade.

"Are you in your first dress?" Her voice carried over the stall, and I heard her unlocking hers.

"Almost." I could barely mask the anxiety that was clouding my every thought.

"What's wrong?" She sounded like she was just outside my door.

Shit.

"Nothing's wrong." I quickly stood and grabbed the first dress I could reach.

"Brooke, open the door." It was a demand, but it was filled with worry and zero command.

I took a deep breath and pulled the door open still dressed in jeans and my t-shirt, one dress crumpled in my hands, the others still hanging on the wall.

"Hey." Sarah stepped into my dressing room, and I didn't even get a chance to tell her how beautiful she looked in her dress. She wrapped her arms around me, crushing the dress in my arms between us, and she ran a hand over the back of my head.

I didn't know what was happening, but I couldn't stop

the emotion that was rushing through me or the way my eyes burned with tears I never shed. This wasn't me. I wasn't this girl.

But here I was in the middle of a dressing room clinging to my fake boyfriend's mom while tears ran down my nose.

"Everything is going to be okay," she whispered the words against my hair, but she didn't know that. Nothing felt like it was going to be okay.

I didn't even know what I was crying for. Everything was going just as we had planned it, and when I got home, Liam was going to help me make my dreams come true.

Nothing else mattered.

I told myself that over and over.

"I know." I nodded into her, but my words didn't even sound believable to me.

She pulled me away from her, just far enough for her to look at me, and she wiped the tears from my face. "You really love him, huh?"

The urge to tell her that wasn't it was overwhelming. But I couldn't do that. It wasn't because of this stupid fake relationship or the things that were relying on my lies.

It was because I didn't think it was a lie at all.

I was an idiot and I was falling for her son.

I nodded my head, and she pulled me tighter against her for a hug. "Everything is going to be okay," she repeated her words. "He loves you too."

Her words hit me like a ton of bricks because she actually believed them. But her son didn't love me. I was a means to an end and I needed to remember that.

Liam wasn't my knight in shining armor. He was just a guy with a secret, and I somehow got lost in it.

CHAPTER 13
LIAM

I had no idea what we were doing.

Last night was the most intimate the two of us had ever been, and it should have had me running away from her as fast as I could go. But I didn't want to.

But she did.

She flew out of my bed this morning as if she had been on fire, and I let her have her space. It was the least that I could do.

Last night felt like too much. It felt like we were breaching a line we were never meant to cross. I should have known better than to ask her to come here, but if I was being honest, I wanted it to be her.

Brooke had been an anomaly to me since the moment I laid eyes on her. She was gorgeous and free and fun, but she was so much more than she let people see. She was more than I knew what to do with.

I could tell by the way she looked at me that things were changing for her. And I wasn't an idiot. I knew they were changing for me too. But that change had to be temporary.

Anything beyond temporary we couldn't handle.

Anything beyond temporary would fuck everything up.

It didn't matter if either of us wanted more. More wasn't what we agreed upon. More was what got you hurt. More was when you gave someone else the power to destroy you, and neither of us wanted to give away that power.

I wasn't sure if I ever would.

But if I did, if she would have been the one, we would have had fun.

Fun was all that I could give her right now.

We only had a couple days left in Tennessee, and I wanted her to enjoy it.

From the moment she walked in the door with my mom, I knew something was wrong. No matter how hard she tried to hide her feelings, her face showed them. But of course as soon as I asked her what was wrong, a smile slipped into place and she assured me that everything was fine.

I didn't believe her for a second.

But she didn't have to tell me her secrets. She didn't owe me anything.

I managed to get her in the car even though alone with me seemed like the last place she wanted to be.

"Just tell me where we're going." She was staring out the window and things felt more tense between us than they ever had before. Even after we almost fucked each other. She avoided me, but it didn't feel like this.

This felt permanent. This felt like she wanted to get as far away from me as she could.

Like there was nothing I could do to change her mind.

"Relax. I promise we're going to have fun." At least I hoped we were.

Today was just going to be me, her, Sophie, and Jase. No

pretending. No fake relationship. Just us. She didn't even have to act like she liked me if she didn't want to.

"I don't trust you." She smiled for the first time since she had been home. The first real smile. "You're probably going to take me back to those swamp waters again."

I rolled my eyes at how ridiculous she was being. "I'm not taking you back to the lake. I learned my lesson the first time."

She turned in her seat to look at me with her brows pinned together. "What's that supposed to mean?"

"Nothing." I held up one hand in defense while driving. "I just don't want to have to balance you on a float all day again so you don't touch the water."

"I touched the water, you jerk. I just don't like swimming where I can't touch. And for your information—" Whatever she was going to say next was cut off as soon as the Ferris wheel came into view.

She sat up straighter in her seat and stared out the windshield like a little kid. She pointed in the direction of the fair with the biggest smile on her face. "Is that where we're going?"

"Yes." I chuckled. "I'm taking it you like the fair?"

She shook her head but didn't take her eyes off the window. "I've never been."

"You've never been to the fair?" I sounded as shocked as I felt. What twenty-something-year-old woman had never been to the fair?

"Nope." She was practically bouncing in her seat as I pulled in. "But I've always wanted to."

She was out of the car before I could cut the engine. She grabbed my hand as I rounded the front without hesitation, almost as if it had become a habit. But I didn't stop her.

I let her pull me toward the entrance, and I couldn't stop smiling at how excited she was. Sophie and Jase were waiting for us at the ticket booth, and that was the icing on the cake. Brooke dropped my hand and practically ran toward Sophie.

I purchased our wristbands while they talked, and Jase leaned against the booth as I handed over my cash.

"So, what's the deal there?" He nodded his head in Brooke's direction.

"You know the deal." I let the ticket lady wrap one of the wristbands around my wrist before I took the other one from her.

"Yeah. I know the agreement the two of you made, but what's really going on there?"

"Nothing." My answer was quick and honest and a complete and total lie.

But I didn't know how to explain something I didn't understand myself. What was I supposed to tell him? I had no damn clue what she was doing to me? I didn't have a clue how I'm supposed to walk away from her when this is all over?

He nodded his head with a grin on his face that told me he didn't believe a word I said. "Whatever you say." He patted my back just as we got to the girls.

I ignored him and held Brooke's wristband out to her. She stuck her arm out, and I held her small wrist in my hand as I wrapped it around.

"You ready?"

She looked up from her wrist and smiled. "I'm so ready."

The place was packed. People were roaming around everywhere, and Brooke was taking it all in like it was the most fascinating place she had ever been.

"What do you want to do first?"

She pointed to some ride that looked like it was made for the sole purpose of making its victims puke, but I followed her anyway.

We climbed inside, and I pulled the metal bar against our laps while Sophie and Jase climbed into the seat in front of us. She was sitting right next to me even though another person could have fit on the other side of her, but I didn't mind.

Actually, I more than didn't mind. I liked it too much.

"I'm a little too excited, huh?" She tucked a piece of stray hair behind her ear and looked away from me.

I put my arm over the back of the seat, around her shoulders, and ran my thumb over the skin there. "No. I think it's cute."

She rolled her eyes, but she couldn't quit smiling. "Cute?"

"What would you prefer I call you? Hot? Gorgeous?"

"Those would be better than cute."

"You already know those things. I don't need to tell you you're gorgeous."

She looked up at me then, really looked at me, and I could tell she hesitated on what she said next. "I don't already know that you think those things."

The ride creaked beneath us, and we started to move as I thought of what to say to her. "You have to know that I think you're beautiful."

She didn't look at me then. She was watching the crowd as we started picking up speed before looking back over her shoulder at me. "You've never told me that. Not when we weren't pretending."

"Any time I tell you you're beautiful, I'm not pretending."

The ride was moving faster and faster and she was all I could see. Everything else was whizzing by us in a blur, but none of it mattered in that moment. I wasn't sure that it ever did.

"You get me?"

She nodded and relaxed a bit into my side. "I get you."

We didn't speak for the rest of the ride. Not that we could even if we wanted to. The ride picked up even more speed, knocking us around in our seat as we spun around. Brooke started laughing beside me.

It started out as a small burst of laughter but soon became uncontrollable as her body slammed into mine from the speed.

I only thought I knew what beautiful was until that moment.

I couldn't help laughing with her. It was contagious and once I started, I couldn't stop. Jace and Sophie were looking back at me like they had never seen me before as we came to a stop, and I couldn't blame them.

There was something about Brooke that made me feel different. Made me act different. There was something about being here with her that was changing everything.

But I didn't care.

I would go back to being the same workaholic asshole I was before all this started, but I would soak up the time we had left as much as I could. If that meant laughing on a ride that was making me nauseous with the girl who was making me question everything, then I would take it.

I wasn't ready to give her up, and I still had the rest of the night before we had to put on another show with the wedding tomorrow.

Then I would tell her that the building was ours, that the

owner accepted the offer while she was gone with my mom this morning, but not tonight. I didn't want tonight to be about the agreement or business or what either of us had at stake. I just wanted it to be about us tonight with nothing at risk.

But I was beginning to see how big of a fool I was.

I was at risk any moment I was with her. I just didn't know it until that moment that she was becoming a risk I was willing to take.

CHAPTER 14
BROOKE

I hadn't had this much fun in forever.

We rode every ride we came across, and Liam bought me every snack we passed. I was on a sugar high, but that didn't stop me from eating the pink cotton candy he held out to me.

The sun was falling behind the mountains and the bright lights of the fair were lighting up the sky.

We were sitting at a small picnic table, taking a break as I stuffed the cotton candy in my mouth, and I was watching this little boy try over and over to win a giant stuffed teddy bear.

He was cute. Probably about seven. His light brown hair was pushed to the side out of his face, and his little face was scrunched in concentration as he threw the football again and missed.

I was pretty positive the game was rigged. The small tire that hung from the rope had the smallest damn opening in the center, and no matter how close he got, the dang ball didn't even consider going through it.

I tore off another piece of cotton candy and watched him. His poor mama had probably already spent twenty dollars on missed throws. I didn't even notice that Liam had got up from our table, not until he was standing beside the boy with a twenty in his hand.

The person behind the stand took his money and put three footballs down in front of him. Liam didn't talk to the little boy and the little boy didn't talk to him, but he was watching him. He watched every step Liam made as he grabbed the football in his hands and lined up his body for the throw.

The first ball hit the center of the tire, but ricocheted off the rubber and landed at the feet of the fair employee. The little boy moved a bit closer to get a better view.

Liam threw it again, this time the ball went directly through the hole. A bunch of little sirens went off and lights within the booth started flashing. The employee smiled and grabbed a teddy bear as big as Liam off a hook. Liam took the bear and set it down at his feet. He still had a ball left.

The boy was staring at his bear, and I couldn't believe that Liam didn't notice him. He could have given him the dang bear and saved his mama the money, but he didn't. He tossed the football in his hands and stared at the tire.

I tore off another piece of cotton candy and stuffed it in my mouth.

Liam looked down at the boy then, and they seemed to study each other while Liam continued to toss the ball. Up and down. Up and down. He nodded his head, motioning in his direction, and the boy took a step closer to him as Liam crouched down.

"What is he doing?" I asked out loud, and I almost forgot

that Sophie and Jase were still at the table until one of them answered.

"It looks like he's giving him a lesson."

I looked over at Jase, and he too was watching his friend.

I couldn't tell what Liam was saying, but the boy kept nodding his head like he understood him. Liam stood and handed the boy the ball. He motioned to his legs, showing the boy how to widen his stance and he followed Liam's every move.

The boy lined up to throw the ball, but Liam stopped him again. He cocked his arm back as if he was getting ready to throw then showed him how to do the same.

This time when the boy threw the ball it almost went in. When it hit the ground, you could see the devastation on his face, but Liam wasn't having any of it. He helped line him back up and grabbed another football for him to throw.

They threw five more balls before one finally went in.

The boy lit up as the booth did the same, and he high-fived Liam with the biggest grin on his face as the employee handed him a matching teddy bear as Liam's. His mom was grinning at them both, and if I couldn't see the pure relief in her eyes, I might have been worried about the way she grabbed Liam's arm and pulled him in a hug.

Liam tousled the boy's hair before grabbing the giant teddy bear and making his way over to us. He had the biggest grin on his face as he made his way toward us, but he tried to hide it.

He held the teddy bear under his arm, but as soon as he stood in front of me, he held it in my direction.

"You win that for me?" I licked some stickiness off my thumb and he watched every second of it.

"What kind of boyfriend would I be if I didn't?" He

reached up and ran his thumb over my bottom lip before setting the giant teddy bear beside me. It was as tall as I was and doubly as round.

Liam squeezed in on the other side of me before snatching some cotton candy out of my hand.

"That was sweet." I nodded toward where the boy and his mom were walking.

"What was?" He acted as if he had no idea what I was talking about, but he knew.

"You know exactly what I'm talking about. Helping that boy."

"It was nothing." He shrugged his shoulders then ignored the conversation altogether. He started talking to Jase about who only knows what, but all I could think about was that boy. It wasn't nothing. Liam was so different than I thought he was. This entire trip had shown me that.

He wasn't some asshole with a chip on his shoulder.

I mean, sure, he could be one, but it all seemed like nothing but a show now. A way to keep others from knowing the truth. I guess we were similar in that way.

He was who he was because he had his heart broken by a girl he thought he was going to love for the rest of his life. I was who I was because the one girl who was meant to love me my entire life was more interested in the men she brought home.

We were so damn different, but somehow I felt like I could still understand him.

I had spent the majority of my life not being good enough.

He had spent his being the star.

My family was broken.

His family was incredible but expected so much from him.

I didn't think he realized how lucky he was.

Even though I should have hated him for taking those things for granted, I didn't. It just made me want to get to know him even more. I wanted to know every little secret he kept from everyone else. I wanted to know exactly what he wanted out of life.

Because from my eyes, he had it all.

An amazing business? Check.

A loving family? Check.

Damn good looks? Double check.

The only thing Liam lacked was the girl, and even though Katie seemed like she was perfect on the outside, I couldn't believe that she was ever right for him.

But I wasn't right for him either.

I was just the girl who was good enough to fake it with him.

He traced his finger over my thigh as he talked to Jase. I wasn't even sure if he knew he was doing it, he seemed so lost in conversation, but I knew.

I tracked every single inch his fingers touched, and I held my breath when they stopped and went the opposite direction.

I was the girl who noticed everything about him, and I wasn't even sure if he knew I was there.

He looked over at me as soon as the thought ran through my head, but I had no idea what he was thinking. His face was as unreadable as always. He was just looking at me with this damn look that could have meant anything.

"You want to ride the Ferris wheel?" His fingers were still trailing over my skin aimlessly.

"Yeah." But I didn't want to move an inch. I didn't want him to stop touching me or looking at me regardless of what it meant.

But he had other plans. He stood, reaching his hand out for me, and I slipped my hand in his and let him lead the way. There was nobody there that I knew besides us, Sophie, and Jase but he still held my hand as we walked toward the giant lit up Ferris wheel.

I could lie to myself and pretend like he was doing it just because he wanted to, but the cold hard reality was that Liam brought me here for a reason. That reason didn't involve my overly wishful thinking or holding hands because he liked the feel of mine in his.

He knew that anyone could see us out here, and we were meant to be dating. Everyone here thought we were more than what we were.

But as much as I repeated those words inside my head, it still didn't feel like it.

He continued to hold my hand as we stood in line, and he didn't let go until it was our turn to climb on.

He climbed in on one side, putting the bear on the other before he patted the seat between them. I squeezed against him, our sides touching from shoulder to knee, and I tried to not think about how warm he was or how good he smelled as the latch came down across our laps.

The Ferris wheel moved slowly, starting and stopping as more riders got on, and Liam was silent next to me for a long time. It felt awkward, and I hated it. I hadn't felt this way with him basically since we had been in Tennessee, but tonight felt different. Without putting on a show, I didn't know how to act. I didn't know what he wanted from me.

And I hated it.

When it came to Liam, I needed clear expectations. Without them, I was just another girl who was going to want more from him than he was willing to give.

We were at the very top with a clear view for miles when Liam reached into his pocket and made the damn thing shake.

"What are you doing?" I held on to the side for dear life.

"Getting this." He pulled a flask out of his pocket and unscrewed the lid before putting it to his lips.

"Are you allowed to have that in here?" I took the flask from his hand and looked around as if someone might catch us way up here in the sky.

"No, but we just can't get caught." He looked so innocent in that moment. He looked like he was nothing more than a boy with a proclivity for trouble, and he made it easy to feel like I was nothing but a girl who was willing to get in it with him.

I took a sip of the strong liquor and wiped my mouth. It burned like hell going down, but I wasn't going to let him know that.

"I bet you can do no wrong in this town."

He smiled at me and took another sip from the flask. "Once upon a time that was true, but I think I've lost my edge."

He handed the drink back to me, and I took it just as the Ferris wheel started to really move. We were spinning around toward the ground then back to the sky, and I couldn't look at anything but him. "I don't think you've lost anything. The women in this town have been clamoring for your attention since you got here."

"I'm not interested in any of the women in this town."

He said it so nonchalantly like it was the simplest statement, but it wasn't simple.

Regardless of what I knew to be true, it made me feel like he wasn't interested in them because he was somehow interested in me, and even though I knew we were fake and I knew everything would eventually go back to normal, I let the alcohol flow through my system and I pressed the flask to my lips once more.

Liam made it easy to pretend to be something I wasn't. He made it easy to pretend that I could be his if only for one night.

I was drunk on the feeling of him, of this night. The alcohol didn't have a thing to do with it, and I never wanted it to end.

...

IT WAS after two in the morning when we finally made it back to the house and made our way up the front stairs. All the lights were off, and I swear I felt like I was sixteen again when Liam held his finger to his lips and shushed me while I giggled.

He pulled his keys out of his pocket and pushed it in the lock before turning the handle slowly. But I was too tipsy to be quiet.

I giggled some more as I pulled my shoes from my feet, and I carried them in my hand as he finally pushed open the front door.

"Are we going to get in trouble?" I whispered, but it sounded a lot louder than a whisper to my own ears.

"If you're not quiet, we are." He shut the door quietly, and I laughed again as I leaned against it.

"This is your fault." I pointed at his chest. "You knew I was loud before you got me drunk then tried to sneak me back in here."

He took a step closer to me, and part of me wished he would just close the space completely.

"Plus, your parents love me. If they get mad at anyone for waking them up, it's going to be you."

"Whose fault is that?" We were practically chest to chest now, and I swear he smelled even better now than he did earlier.

How was that even possible?

"Yours." I pushed my finger into his chest, and he caught it. "You're the one who brought me here. I can't help it that you weren't expecting everyone to fall for me."

"You're right."

"So you're admitting that it's your fault?"

"No." He shook his head. "I'm admitting I didn't expect for you to be so easy to fall for." He didn't give me the time to process what he had just said. Instead, he pushed even closer to me and ran his nose along the length of my neck. "I didn't expect for any of this to happen." His words were a whisper, but they echoed through me as if he'd screamed them.

We were tiptoeing over the edge, and I didn't know where we should stop. I didn't know how to cross that line without being hurt. I didn't know how to cross it and ever get back to what we were when we went home.

Because we would be going home, and this all would end. Every part of it, and I didn't know where I would stand.

Would we go back to being friends who barely spoke to each other? Would we somehow be more?

He linked his fingers with mine before taking a step back toward the stairs. I followed him, his hand not letting me go, and I couldn't help but smile when he held his finger to his lips signaling for me to be quiet. We tiptoed up the steps hand in hand, and when Liam almost tripped over the top step, a laugh bubbled out of me.

We ran past his parents' bedroom door, both of us laughing, and I dropped his hand along with my shoes the moment he shut his bedroom door.

"My mom might not love you so much anymore if she knew you were sneaking us into the house so late at night and trying to seduce her sweet, innocent boy."

My mouth dropped open as he leaned against the small desk that sat in the corner of his room.

"You are not sweet and innocent."

"So you are trying to seduce me?" He arched a brow at me, and I knew he was teasing me. But his room was dark and the alcohol was still running through my system, and I wanted nothing more than to get under his skin.

I wanted to get under his skin like he managed to do to me every day without even trying. I wanted to make him regret every time he ever thought we were a bad idea. I wanted him to want me as badly as I wanted him.

"Do you think this is me seducing you?" I sat down on the end of his bed. "I'm doing a pretty piss-poor job. Don't you think?" I cocked my head to the side and stared at him.

"I don't know. It seems to be working to me."

I rummaged through my bag at the end of the bed and pulled out my pajamas. I popped the button on my shorts and Liam's gaze was glued to the movement. "You've made it abundantly clear that you don't want me, Liam. No need for this little game." I lifted my ass and pulled my shorts down my legs while he watched.

"When the fuck did I make that clear?"

His words made my skin boil. He knew exactly when he had made that clear.

"I don't know. Maybe the hundred times you've pushed me away or the time you ate me out then forgot about it the second it happened like it was the least memorable thing to ever happen to you." I was angry now. Just thinking about that night pissed me off.

He was in my face so quickly, I didn't have a second to hide my reaction. But I didn't care. I was tired of pretending that he didn't bother me. I was tired of pretending that the way he seemed interested in every girl but me didn't hurt.

"I didn't forget a single second of it. I think about that night every time I see you, every time you walk away, and I definitely think about that night when I'm alone with my cock in my hand."

"So, what? I'm the girl you think about when you have nobody else to take care of you?" I grazed my fingers over his zipper, and he let out a growl. It made my heart race even faster and my stomach tighten.

"I haven't been with anyone since that night I was with you. You're all I've been able to think about for the last two months."

His words were shocking and unfair and more importantly a lie. Liam didn't think about me.

He didn't get to pretend like I suddenly mattered to him.

"You haven't thought about me." I stated the fact that we both already knew. "You're only thinking about me now because you need me."

"Don't tell me what I'm thinking." He pushed closer to

me, my hand firm against his groin. "You don't have a fucking clue what's going through my head."

He was right, but that was only because he made it that way. He's the one who always kept me at arm's length. He was the one who didn't want this.

"Then show me."

As soon as the words left my lips, his mouth crashed down against mine. It wasn't gentle or smooth. This was no longer the Liam that he let everybody see. He was messy and unrestrained, and I loved it.

His teeth hit mine, his lips swallowed my moan, and just when I thought I knew what he was going to do next, he sucked my tongue into his mouth before biting down on the tip. He didn't talk as he pressed a knee into the mattress or as he used his hands under my arms to lift me farther up the bed.

He had me exactly where he wanted me, and I wouldn't dare move a muscle. I was too scared that one wrong move would make him stop. One wrong move and he would regret what he started.

There wasn't a trace of hesitation in his touch as he pushed my shirt up my stomach and traced the movement with his tongue. He nipped my belly button, making my back arch off the bed, but he didn't stop. He continued his path until my shirt was above my chest and his mouth was still pressed against my skin.

He didn't stop as he tasted the edge of my breast or when he jerked my bra to the side so he could run his tongue over my nipple.

I pulled my t-shirt the rest of the way off, eager for him to have full access to my body, but he caught me last minute, trapping my hands above my head.

He didn't look up or even acknowledge the hold he had on me, but I could feel it. I felt the way his fingers were digging into my wrists all the way to my toes, and I thought I was going to die if he didn't do something more.

"Liam." His name was a plea, but I didn't know what I was asking for.

Something. Anything.

He looked up at me then, his gaze holding mine as he spoke with his lips still pressed against my nipple. "What do you want, baby?"

"I don't know." I shook my head, but I didn't dare move my gaze away from his. He was too mesmerizing, and I didn't know if I would ever get to see him this way again.

"Yes. You do." He moved down my body, still holding my gaze, and he stared at me as he flicked his tongue against my panties.

I wasn't a prude or some damn virgin who didn't know what she was doing. I knew what I wanted when it came to sex, but when it came to Liam, it was different. I didn't even have my damn panties off, and he already had me panting his name.

There was something about him that threw me off. He made me feel like I didn't have a clue what I was doing, and the only thing that was running through my mind was more.

Whatever he was going to give me, I wanted more.

I shook the t-shirt off my wrists and sat up on my elbows as he tugged my panties down my legs. I half expected him to spread me open, to dive into me without any thought, but that wasn't Liam's style. He was calculated and teasing, and every move he made was driving me insane.

He pushed my legs together, placing his on either side of them, and he lightly ran his tongue along the seam of my pussy. Somehow that barely-there touch did more for me than any touch from any man before him.

He slid his tongue inside slowly. Every part of me wanted to force my legs open for him, but he wasn't having any of it. He was in complete control, and from the look on his face, he was enjoying watching me struggle. I never gave control away during sex. Even if it was just him forcing my thighs together.

I felt like he knew it too. He knew that I was about to tell him that I didn't want him to have it. As soon as I opened my mouth to tell him to let my legs go, his tongue moved over my clit and he sucked. My legs jerked beneath him, but they no longer gave a shit about where they were.

Everything inside of me just wanted more more more.

He continued sucking while alternating flicks of his tongue, and I had never had my pussy eaten like this before. The position he forced me into made me feel everything with more intensity. Every single touch was purposeful. Every swipe of his tongue meant to destroy me.

His hands moved from my thighs, up over my hips, and his fingers dug into my flesh as he held me down against the bed. I bit down on my forearm, trying like hell not to cry out as my orgasm raced through me. It was rapid and all-consuming, and Liam didn't stop until he milked every ounce of pleasure from my body.

Just as I caught my breath, he flipped me over onto my stomach and ran his nose along my spine. He was still fully dressed behind me, and I was in nothing but my disheveled bra. It felt fitting somehow. He always seemed to have the advantage between us, and here I was once again, laying vulnerable before him.

"You are perfect."

I could barely make out his words as he kissed the small of my back, but I heard them. Regardless of what he meant, those three words rang through me as I heard his zipper behind me.

I looked over my shoulder and he was staring down at me. He reached behind his neck, gripping his shirt in his hand, and he pulled it over his head in one quick movement. I didn't dare take my eyes off him.

He pulled his cock out of his jeans, and he stared down at my ass as he ran it back and forth against me. I let out a soft moan as he hit my still sensitive pussy.

He gripped my hips in his hands and jerked me to my knees in one quick motion. I held my body up on my elbows, and Liam lined himself up behind me.

I half expected him to ask me if I was sure about this or if I wanted to change my mind, but he did neither. He was too far gone for any of that, and I was too far gone to stop him.

I would never stop him.

I could feel him pressed against me, and I looked down at my hands as I tried to stop myself from begging him to hurry. Every part of my body felt like it was a live wire.

"Look at me." His command was soft but forceful, and I didn't hesitate to look over my shoulder at where he stood. One of his hands was on my ass, spreading me open for him, and the other was lining himself up. "Your eyes stay on me."

He didn't wait for my answer. Instead, he pushed inside of me, and I fought to keep my eyes open as my body adjusted to him.

He pushed into me slowly before pulling back out, and he was watching where our bodies connected as he pushed in and out. After a moment of adjusting, his hands moved to my hips and he slammed into me with a force that slammed the bed into the wall.

"Oh God." I felt so full, so incredibly full, and I pushed back against him because I still craved more.

His pace picked up, and my elbows slipped out from under me. I buried my forehead against my hands just as one of his hands wrapped around the back of my neck. He continued to pound into me as his hand tightened, and I could feel myself tightening around him.

"Liam." My body was thrumming, and I felt the need for something. I needed to touch him, to see him, for him to talk to me, something. I just needed to know that he was in this with me and felt as crazy with lust as I did.

He lifted me, pulling my back to his chest without disconnecting us, and his hand on my neck moved around to the front. His grip was light, but he held me exactly where he wanted me, and I sat against him, the position making him feel impossibly deep.

His lips pressed against my neck where his fingers were still holding me as I started moving against him, and his other hand snaked down my body until it felt where our bodies were connected. I could feel his hand against me, his fingers spreading me open as he pushed in and out of me, and the heel of his hand started working in small hard circles against my clit.

"Fuck." My head slammed back against his shoulder, and he took advantage of the angle and swallowed my moans with his mouth.

"Shhh." The sound vibrated against our lips. "You don't want to wake up my parents."

Shit. I had completely forgotten about them. How the hell had I forgotten that they were just down the hall?

"Wait." There was no way in hell I wanted them to wake up to the sound of their son fucking me.

"It's not fucking happening, baby." He kissed me again and the panic that was starting to rise only a second before was completely forgotten. "I need to feel you come on me."

He pushed up inside me harder, and I knew that I was almost there. There was no way that I wanted him to stop.

"Liam."

The heel of his hand pressed harder against me as I cried out and reached behind me, holding on to his thigh with one hand and grabbing his arm with the other as my orgasm coursed through my body.

I fell apart around him, and he held me against him as he continued to thrust inside. I could feel his body tense, and I tightened around him as he said my name.

He followed me over the edge in the next moment. He came inside me, and I had a moment of panic as I realized for the first time that we hadn't used a condom.

But what made me panic more was that I didn't care.

Liam turned my face toward his and he kissed me. He kissed me like he couldn't get enough of me, like I was the thing he always wanted, and I kissed him back just as hard.

I didn't know what tomorrow would hold, and if this was going to be my only moment with him, I was going to take advantage of every second of it.

I turned toward him as he slipped out of me, and I wrapped my arms around his neck. I kept my eyes closed as I kissed him. I wasn't ready for this to end. I wasn't ready for reality to take over and ruin what just happened.

I didn't want to see a single trace of regret on his face.

His hands ran over my head, and he pushed my hair back out of my face. His hands were gentle and caressing, and if I didn't know any better, it would feel like tonight meant as much to him as it did to me.

He peppered kisses against my jaw, my lips, my nose, and I finally opened my eyes to find him looking down at me with a look I couldn't decipher.

Neither one of us said anything. Liam laid back on his bed, his head hitting the pillow, before he pulled me forward until my chest fell into his.

He pulled a blanket over us, neither one of us worried about cleaning up or getting dressed, and I snuggled down against him. I would deal with the repercussions tomorrow. We both would. But tonight, tonight I was going to soak up everything he was willing to give.

And I didn't regret a thing.

CHAPTER 15
LIAM

She looked absolutely gorgeous.

Today had been a whirlwind of activity.

We had barely had a moment to talk, and I had no idea where her head was at.

We had overslept this morning, and she jumped out of my bed like she was on fire when my mom called through the door that they were going to be late for their nail appointment.

Apparently, the two of them took the wedding as an excuse to go all out. They had an appointment to get their nails done then their hair, and I was thankful. My mama needed a day of pampering. She never did that for herself.

But I was still worried as hell about what was going through Brooke's head.

She scurried around the room throwing clothes on and tossing her hair into a bun, and I could see the panic on her face as I watched her from the bed. Was she panicking because they were late or was the regret from last night starting to hit her full force?

I couldn't tell, but I knew that I didn't feel an ounce of it. If I regretted anything, it was that I had ever pushed her away.

Being with Brooke was far more than I expected.

Everything about her was. Last night was more than just sex. Bringing her here was more than just a fucking deal that the two of us made.

I had never wanted to please a woman as eagerly as I had last night. Never had my own pleasure been so dependent on someone else, and even though I probably should have hated it, I didn't.

I just wanted more.

She had tried to run from the room without a word or even a sideways glance, but I wasn't having any of that shit. I grabbed her hand and tugged her toward me, and she fell into my chest as a loud huff left her mouth. I didn't care if she was late or if she was confused or irritated. There was no way in hell that she was leaving my room without me getting another small taste of her.

I pressed my lips against hers before she could object, and her body melted against me. I could feel half of the anxiety leaving her body, and I hated that I had made her feel this way. If I treated her better before, she would never be questioning what I wanted from her now.

She glanced up at me with so much hesitation still in her eyes before she pushed away from me and left the room without a word.

And I was going crazy.

I knew what last night felt like to me, but I had no idea what she was feeling. We had both been drinking, not that I was blaming our decisions on the alcohol because I would live last night again over and over. But would she?

Here she was already spending a week of her life with me to what? Lie to my fucking parents because I couldn't just admit that I hadn't found anyone that interested me in the least? Well, that was a lie. Brooke had always interested me.

I had just been too big of a fool to realize it.

But staring at her now at this wedding, where she laughed next to my mom with her blond hair curled and pushed back out of her face, I couldn't believe that I hadn't seen it before.

I was a damn idiot.

I leaned toward her and whispered in her ear. "Want to dance?"

She looked at me over her shoulder, a smile still on her face from whatever she and my mom were talking about, and she nodded instantly.

Her hand slipped into mine as I stood, and I pulled her along with me to the dance floor. She had on a floor-length green dress, and it fit her body like it was made for her. Her shoulders were bare and still kissed from the sun from her time here in Tennessee, and I suddenly realized that her shoulders were my favorite part of her body. It was weird. I had never been attracted to someone's shoulders before, but with her I was. I was attracted to everything. Every single inch of her.

She wrapped one hand behind my neck and pressed the other to my chest as I pulled her against me.

"Have I told you how beautiful you are?"

She rolled her eyes playfully as I moved us around the floor. "Only like a hundred times. Was the sex that good?"

She grinned and I knew this was her way of trying to not

make a big deal of what happened last night, and I would let her have it.

"It was." I nodded and tightened my hand on the small of her back as I spoke only for her to hear. "Who knew we'd be that good together?"

I felt a tiny shiver run through her body, and it made me want to rip that damn dress off her body and take her right there. I could practically see the thoughts running through her head. She was trying to think of what to say to me. The clever, witty Brooke McCarter was so good at deflecting, but I didn't want her to deflect this. I wanted her to admit that last night was more than just amazing sex for her.

I wanted her to admit that she was feeling as crazy as I was.

"I had a feeling. Those hands can't be that good with a football but completely terrible in the bedroom."

But I was the one who put us here. I was the one who had drawn the line in the sand and told her that she was nothing more than this. This fun girl who I could be friends with and ask to come to my parents but not anything more.

I was the one who had proved exactly what she was worth when it came to me, and I was bound and determined to make sure she knew how wrong I was.

And it wasn't the sex.

It was the way she laughed without abandon and the way she treated my mom like she had loved her her entire life. It was the way she was meant to come here and be my fake girlfriend, but there wasn't a thing about her that was fake.

It was the way she lingered.

From the moment I met her, every encounter had lingered like she was a mystery I just couldn't solve. She was always there. Sometimes in the back of my mind, sometimes front and center where I couldn't avoid thinking about her, but no matter what, she always lingered.

I spun her around, catching her off guard, and she giggled as the bottom of her dress swirled around her in a circle.

"I think it was more than my hands." I quickly pressed my lips against hers before I could convince myself otherwise. "I love it when you laugh like that."

"Like what?"

She always had this dreaming look in her eyes after I kissed her. It didn't matter if it had been for show or for real. She always looked like I had just given her the best kiss of her life.

"Like you don't give a fuck who's watching you." I looked around the room, and sure enough, there were several sets of eyes on us. I used to think they were all watching just waiting for me to screw up, but now they were all watching her. She didn't notice. "You never seem to care."

"Oh. I care." She moved her hand up and down the lapel of my jacket. "I just refuse to give them the satisfaction of seeing me care."

"You're good at it." I couldn't stop staring at her mouth. "The only thing I'm one hundred percent certain that you care about is Kennedy."

She looked away from me but turned back quickly with irritation clouding her face. "You don't think I care about you?"

"Do you?" I whispered, but my question was loud and clear.

"Fuck you, Liam." She tried to pull away from me, but I refused to let her go. I was so damn tired of letting her go.

She pushed against my chest but I tightened my hold. She looked up at me, really good and angry now, and even though I wished we could have had this conversation without it, I welcomed her anger. It was the only time I could really read her.

"You know I care about you."

"I do." I moved my hand from her hip to her elbow, and she tensed as I ran my fingers along the back of her arm. "But how much do you care about me?"

She pressed her lips together and stared at me. We were both so damn stubborn. Neither one of us were willing to put ourselves at risk. Neither one of us willing to jump alone.

"Why does it matter, Liam?" She looked around the room at all the people who surrounded us. Everyone was still on a high from the wedding, and the bride and groom were dancing just a few steps away. "All of this will be over soon." She looked back to me. "It doesn't matter what I care about."

She was so damn wrong.

It was the only thing that mattered.

"When we get home, everything will go back to the way it was, and you won't have to worry about whether I care or not. Everyone here already believes it."

"What if I don't want it to go back to the way it was?" I couldn't breathe as she stared up at me.

"I don't know." She shook her head gently. "I don't know." She looked away from me and I had no clue what she was going to say next. "What about us working together?"

"What about it?" We were barely dancing now, but I didn't care.

"What if we decide that things don't have to go back to normal then we work together and things don't work out?

Then what? You'll have a building and I'll be left with nothing."

I winced as if she had slapped me. "You really think I would do that to you?"

"No." She shook her head quickly, and I could tell that she regretted her words. "I just don't want to end up with nothing."

I cupped her cheek in my hand. "I wouldn't do that."

I could tell she wanted to trust me from the way she was looking at me, but I wasn't asking for her to make a decision right now. That wasn't fair.

Nothing I asked of her was.

I twirled her around again, and she smiled even though it didn't meet her eyes.

"He accepted our offer."

"What?" She leaned away from me slightly and stared me straight in the eye.

I nodded my head. "My real estate agent sent over some paperwork earlier. He finally accepted."

I couldn't tell if she was mad that I had waited until now to tell her or if she was happy. Either way, she just stared at me without saying a word.

"That's what we wanted, right?" Now I was second-guessing myself. I was second-guessing every decision I ever made with her.

"Yes." She snapped out of whatever haze she was just in, and her hand gripped my forearm. "Are you kidding me? Yes." A laugh bubbled out of her.

She had the biggest smile on her face as she wrapped her arms around my neck and pulled me into a hug. She laughed again and I couldn't stop myself from joining her. People were looking at us, but it didn't matter.

"I can't believe this is happening." Her words were mumbled against me.

I kissed the top of her head. "It's happening."

She looked up at me and rose on her tiptoes. I couldn't look anywhere but at her. She threaded her fingers through my hair, pulling me down to meet her, and she stared at my mouth as she said, "Thank you."

She didn't wait for me to respond. She pulled me harder into her and her lips met mine. She kissed me like I was responsible for every bit of happiness she ever felt.

She leaned back, still hanging on to me, and she looked like every worry she ever had been lifted from her shoulders.

"Do you want some champagne?" I couldn't stop smiling at her.

"I'd love some."

I reached for her hands and held them in mine. I didn't want to let her go. I didn't want to lose this moment or this feeling or the way she was looking at me.

I didn't want her to look at me any other way.

I brought her hand to my mouth and kissed her soft inner wrist. "I'm going to go grab us some then we can celebrate."

"Okay." She nodded. "I'm going to run to the ladies' room."

I let go of her hands and she was still smiling as she walked away from me.

I decided in that moment that no matter what she decided she wanted from me, I was going to make it my mission to keep that look on her face. Even if it meant that we were nothing but business partners. Even if she wanted nothing else from me.

I walked to the bar and ordered us both a glass of champagne.

. . .

"Hey there, stranger." I looked down at Katie as she tucked a piece of hair behind her ear as she leaned against the bar next to me while I waited for mine and Brooke's order, and even though I hated the fact, I could still admit she looked beautiful tonight.

Her brown hair was tied in a braid down one shoulder and she wore a simple blue dress that fit her perfectly.

"Hi." I looked back to the bar. I didn't have the time or energy it took to deal with Katie, and all I wanted was to grab our drinks and get back to Brooke.

"Do you have a second?" She looked around before looking back at me.

I couldn't imagine what in the world she could possibly have to say to me, but even though the girl didn't deserve it, I couldn't just be an ass to her.

"How have you been?" She looked like she was genuinely curious and that just pissed me off. She didn't have any right to be curious about me anymore.

"I've been good. Really good." I nodded my head. "How about you?"

From what I heard, she hadn't done much with her life since I've been gone beyond moving into Brad's house and waiting on his every whim. That wasn't the girl I knew. It wasn't the girl I had loved.

"I've been okay." She looked at her feet, and I could feel her nerves rolling off of her. I had always been able to read her so easily.

"That's good." There was a long moment of awkward silence, and I wished she would use it as an excuse to walk away, but she didn't.

Instead, she took a small step closer to me as if she wouldn't dare let anyone else hear what she was about to say. "I'm sorry, you know? I'm really sorry."

Hell, she may have been, but I still didn't believe her. I didn't think I would ever be able to believe the words that came out of her mouth again.

"How's Brad?" I knew my words hurt her as soon as I said them, but I didn't care. Despite the fact that everything between us happened years ago, I was still allowed to not give a shit.

"He's okay." Her voice was even softer now. "I would take it back if I could." She stared up at me, and I could see the sincerity in her eyes. "I would take it all back."

"But you can't." She couldn't take any of it back. Not a second of it, and she had to live with the choices she made. We both did.

"I know." She looked behind her like she was worried Brad would see her talking to me, and when she turned back toward me every bit of emotion she was just showing was locked down so tight it was easy to remember how I once had believed all her lies. "I just wanted you to know that I would."

She took a step toward me, and for a quick moment, the urge to reach out to her was overwhelming. But that was nothing more than an old habit. I didn't want Katie anymore, and the only person who flashed into my head at that moment was Brooke.

"I would give anything to have us back."

I stared down at her, and I couldn't believe she was saying this to me. After all this time, at the worst place possible.

"I'm with someone else." I grabbed the two flutes of

champagne the bartender set in front of me and started to walk away, but I could feel Katie right on my heels.

"I know about her." Her words were soft, but they held their impact.

I turned around quickly, tucking the two of us out of sight from the rest of the wedding, and I could barely control my anger.

"You don't know a thing about her."

"Yes. I do." She nodded her head, and I could see the fire in her eyes. "I know that you two aren't really together. I know that you paid her to be here."

I flinched as if she had hit me. I didn't pay Brooke to be here. Not really. Did I offer her an opportunity she couldn't refuse? Sure. But she wasn't some prostitute like Katie made her sound.

"You have no idea what you're talking about, Katie."

She reached out and grabbed my arm as I tried to walk away. "I overheard her talking about it, Liam. What would your mom think?"

"My mom isn't going to find out."

"She doesn't have to."

"Don't fucking threaten me, Katie." I took a step into her space. "Does Brad know you're over here asking me for another chance? Does he know that you care as little about him as you did about me?"

"I loved you." She genuinely seemed hurt by my words, but I had already spent too much time in my life worried about her and her feelings. She put her hand on my chest, and I stared down at where she was touching me.

"There you are." I took a step back from Katie as soon as I heard Brooke's voice. "Oh. I'm sorry."

She stared at Katie but didn't make eye contact with me

as she quickly turned back in the direction she came from and walked away from us.

"Brooke." She didn't stop when I called out to her, and I couldn't stand the idea of her thinking I was back here with Katie while she was waiting for me.

I took a step toward her. I didn't give a shit what else Katie had to say. I walked away from her as easily as she had me all those years ago, and I rushed through the crowd to get to Brooke. I couldn't stand the thought of her thinking I would ever choose Katie over her.

That I would ever hurt in that way even if we were just pretending.

If she was pretending. Because I wasn't. Not anymore.

"Brooke." I reached out and gripped her fingers in mine. "Hold on."

She turned toward me, and I could see the panic in her eyes before she quickly hid it. "I didn't mean to interrupt you." She looked over my shoulder to where Katie and I just were.

"You weren't interrupting anything."

"It looked like I was." She didn't say it like she was accusing me. She said it like she was sad.

"She wanted to talk."

"It's okay, Liam," she interrupted me before I could explain. "You don't owe me an explanation."

But I did. I owed her more than I would ever be able to give her.

She nodded toward the table where my parents sat. "I'm going to get some air before I head back over there." She lifted the skirt of her dress so she wouldn't step on it and started moving away from me.

"I'll come with you."

"No." The word was so sure. So final. "I just need a minute alone."

I didn't want to give her a minute alone. I didn't want to give a single second.

She knew it too. "Please, Liam." She took another step back from me, and I swear I could see pain in her eyes.

Pain that I had caused her without even trying.

I didn't want to hurt her anymore.

"Okay." I nodded my head. If this was what she needed then it was what I'd give her.

Her blond hair was still perfectly curled and the dress still fit her body like a glove, but that spark in her eyes that she walked in with, that was completely gone.

"I'll meet you back at the table." I nodded toward where my parents still sat. Not a clue in the world that their son was losing the girl he never even had.

But I could feel it.

She was pulling away from me right in front of my eyes.

CHAPTER 16
BROOKE

I felt like I couldn't breathe.

I knew that was silly. I had no right to be mad, and I wasn't. I was something that I couldn't even explain.

I was confused and hurt and so damn mad at myself for ever thinking this was more than it actually was.

Liam didn't do anything wrong. He was kind to me and playful, and I let my stupid heart lead instead of my head.

I never let that happen, and there was a reason.

This was the reason.

I had no idea what he and Katie were talking about, and I didn't have a right to know.

But it didn't matter.

I saw the way he was looking at her. It was the same way he looked at her every time we saw her. He looked at her like he would never look at me.

Katie had been real for him.

I was a business deal.

Regardless of what he thought he felt.

And I needed to start acting like one.

I needed to remember that Liam was acting and regardless of how good of an actor he was, I was a complete fool if I didn't remember exactly where I stood. Tonight was nothing but a reminder of that.

He was caught up in this week and what he thought he wanted, but we would be going back home tomorrow and reality would hit him.

He would regret believing we could be anything more.

I was going to be his business partner, and as such, I had no right to care about what he was doing with his ex. I had no right to care that her hand had been on his chest like he was hers.

He had been more hers than he had ever been mine.

She was the only one who had any right to care or be jealous, but she gave up that right the moment she chose anyone else over him.

I hated her for hurting him and being here and making me question everything just when I thought I had a clue about what I was feeling.

I stared out over the small balcony at the small creek that ran by the hotel. The wedding had been beautiful. Liam's cousin didn't look a thing like him, but he did look happy.

He looked so in love with his bride that it made me a bit jealous. I was dying to be looked at like that.

I was an idiot.

I was an idiot for coming here, for ever agreeing to this whole damn plan of Liam's, and I was an idiot for letting myself forget why I was here.

I took a deep breath and straightened my shoulders. I had faked my way through far worse situations than this one. I just had to be the doting girlfriend for one more day then I could go home where no one else could see me, and I would let myself fall apart.

Walking back into the reception, my eyes immediately sought out Liam. He was sitting at our table next to his parents and some other people he introduced me to but I couldn't remember their names. His dad was talking to him, but Liam looked stressed.

He looked up at me as soon as I came in view, and I smiled at his parents so they wouldn't know that anything was wrong. They were what I was here for, and no matter how much I hated lying to them, especially his mom, I only had one more day of this left.

"Brooke," Liam said my name like he wanted to talk, but this wasn't the place or the time.

I pushed up onto my tiptoes and kissed his cheek before taking a seat next to his mom. He was still staring at me, and I didn't know what he wanted from me. I didn't know what he expected.

If I just didn't care then everything would be easier. If I didn't care then everything would have gone just like it was supposed to.

"Everything okay?" His mom put her hand over mine.

"Of course." I smiled at her but I didn't think she believed it. I didn't believe it.

She ran her fingers over my skin, and she gave me a sad smile. It almost broke me.

I could deal with me getting hurt, but I didn't know how I was going to handle it when she did.

Not when I was the one to cause it.

The two of us had the best day today. We got our nails done and our hair styled, and I laughed so hard with her that my stomach hurt. It made me wish that she was mine. My mother was nothing like his, and I hated that I had to give her up.

Things wouldn't just be going back to normal with me and Liam when we left. There would be no more Sarah. No more Jim.

They were his.

And I wasn't.

"Ladies and gentlemen, please help me welcome the bride and groom to the dance floor for the final dance." The DJ's voice rang through the speakers and dread filled me.

I wasn't ready to go back to Liam's parents' house.

I wasn't ready to be alone with him. I didn't want to talk about what happened tonight. I didn't want to explain why I was affected at all.

"Do you want to dance?" Liam was at my side and he was looking at me like he would give anything for me to say yes, but I couldn't.

"I'm really tired." I avoided his eyes as I said the words. It wasn't a lie. I felt like I could sleep for a week and still be exhausted.

"Okay." He nodded in understanding, but he didn't. "Let's go." He reached for my hand and I let him take it as he pulled me to my feet.

We told his parents we'd see them at the house then we walked out to the car in complete silence. Still hand in hand.

I could tell he was thinking about what to say to me, but he just kept stewing. I was thankful. If we could just avoid this conversation altogether, I would be happy.

We didn't need to hash this out. It would only make things more complicated, and that was the last thing we needed.

I stared out the car window as he drove us home, and I

could practically feel the tension buzzing between us. I just wanted to get back to the house, take off this dress, and bury my head in my pillow.

He cut off the engine and took a loud breath. "I don't know what you think you saw back there, but Katie means nothing to me."

I looked down at my lap. "It's fine, Liam." I tried to change the subject. "Are you going to tell me how much the building cost? I know I probably can't contribute half, but I should be contributing something."

"The damn building isn't important." He sounded frustrated with me, but I was frustrated with him.

I opened the car door and took a deep breath of the fresh air. I felt like everything was closing in on me. "Yes. It is. It's the only thing that matters."

I climbed out of the car before he could respond, but he was right behind me.

"That's such bullshit and you know it." He rounded the car, but I was already headed for the house. "Brooke, talk to me."

I spun in his direction, and I could feel my throat getting tight. "What do you want me to say?"

"I don't know." He threw his arms out to the side. "But something other than this bullshit. Don't pretend you're only in this for the deal."

"What do you think I'm in this for, Liam?" I marched up the stairs and waited at the door until he opened it. "We had a deal with clear rules."

He opened the door and motioned for me to go inside. "I think we blew those rules out of the fucking water last night, don't you?"

I didn't wait for him or turn around to see if he was

following me as I stomped up the stairs. These damn heels were killing my feet, and I wasn't going to stand around arguing with him in four-inch heels. I opened his bedroom door and started unclasping the small buckle around my ankle. "Last night was a mistake. Neither one of us should have let it happen. We shouldn't have screwed this up."

"It wasn't a mistake." He was standing directly behind me, and I hated how wounded he sounded.

"This can't work." I motioned between the two of us.

"Why not?"

"Because." I didn't know what to say. He knew we were a bad idea as much as I did. "We're barely even friends, Liam."

"We've seemed like pretty good friends since we've been in Tennessee." He threw his suit jacket on his small desk.

"Isn't that what you hired me to do?" I crossed my arms and tried to breathe. I needed to end this now. I was already hurt and we hadn't even started. Liam was the kind of guy that could destroy me. I couldn't rely on him for everything. I came here because of what he offered me. Regardless of how badly I didn't want to be like my mom, I knew that.

But I refused to give him all the power over me. I refused to let him hold my heart in his hands and trust that he wouldn't crush it whenever he realized I wasn't what he wanted.

"I think I've played the part perfectly."

He looked at me like he barely knew me, and I hated it. I wanted to wrap my arms around his neck and beg him to forget everything I had said.

But Liam deserved better than that. He deserved more than I could give him.

He moved toward me, the smell of his cologne enough to

make me want to reach out and touch him, but he wasn't waiting for me. He gripped my chin in his hand and forced me to look up at him.

"If you want to pretend like that's all this is, then let's pretend." His hand moved from my jaw to the back of my head. "One more night." My hair tightened in his fingers, and even though I wished it hadn't, a small moan fell from my lips. "Make me believe that I'm nothing to you."

He let go of my hair, and I could barely catch my breath as he started unbuttoning his shirt. This was a bad idea. The worst idea we had yet, but I couldn't say no.

I wanted him too badly. I wanted him to take away tonight and make me forget that this was all coming to an end. I wanted him to make me forget that we weren't real even if that's what he wanted me to prove.

He jerked his shirt from his shoulders as I bunched my dress around my hips. He was staring at me like he hated me, and I welcomed it. I could deal with him hating me. I could deal with the cold, impassive Liam I knew before we ever came to this godforsaken state.

I pulled my dress over my head and he unbuckled his belt. He was standing in front of me in only his dress pants and shoes, and he looked beautiful. He looked like he could have anyone he wanted, and I knew it was true. I knew that he had made me fall for him even though I didn't want to.

This wasn't who I was. I was the girl who could detach everything. Sex was sex and a business deal was a business deal, but somehow everything got completely mixed up.

"Get on your knees, Brooke." His words were a command, and I fell to my knees as he closed the space between him. I didn't let any men boss me around, but this didn't feel like that. This felt like he wouldn't survive if I didn't do what he asked, and I found myself eager to please him.

He stood in front of me, and I quickly released the button on his pants before pulling down his zipper. He shifted his pants down his body, just enough for his cock to come free, and I looked up at him as I took it in my hand. He was staring down at me with a fire I had never felt before, and I didn't dare look away as I ran my tongue over the length of him and buried him in my mouth.

His hands found their way back to my hair, and I moaned around him at the edge of pleasure and pain his hands brought. He wasn't fucking around. He let me keep control as I took him in and out of my mouth as far as he could go, but he didn't let me forget who truly held the power.

He ran one of his thumbs over my bottom lip before he slammed into my mouth. My eyes watered because I wasn't prepared, but I didn't dare stop him. His grip tightened in my hair as he started to really fuck my face, and I watched his features as the pleasure took over.

Last night had been about me, but this right here. This was for him, and I would give it to him. I would give it to him a hundred times over if it meant that I wouldn't hurt him. If it meant that we could go back to us and not have a new awkwardness between us that would only remind me of what could have been.

If I wasn't such a fool.

"I'm going to come," he growled out as his hands tightened in my hair, but I refused to let him stop. I continued to move against him, against the pain from where his hands were attempting to pull me away, and I stared up at him just as he came against the back of my throat.

He came hard and his face was riddled with pain and pleasure, and I wondered if he could see the same look in my eyes. If he knew how much all of this was killing me.

He gripped me just below my breasts and pulled me up against him. I was barely on my toes as he held me, but I had no fear of falling. His hold was firm and unyielding, and I never wanted him to let me go.

He pressed his lips to mine, his kiss in complete contrast to the way he ravished my mouth only moments before, and I hated that him being this way with me could break me. Him being gentle and caring and kissing me like I might break would be the thing that did just that. It would be the thing that made me fall apart.

His lips moved from my lips to my jaw and down my neck and he kissed me as if he was trying to memorize every curve of my body. He kissed me as if he knew this would be the last time.

"Liam." I couldn't do this. I couldn't have him be this way with me and still walk away.

"Don't." His lips were back on mine, and he backed me up against the wall as he kissed the fight out of me. Whatever chance I had of denying him was gone.

His hands wrapped around my thighs and he lifted me off the ground. I immediately wrapped my legs around his hips as my back pressed into the wall. He was pressed into me as if he feared I would try to escape, but I still wanted more.

I ground against him, my panties still in the way, and he groaned in my mouth.

"You drive me crazy." He shoved my panties to the side, not even bothering with pulling them down my legs, and he pushed into me like he couldn't take another second without it.

I held on to his shoulders and pressed my head against the wall. I watched him as he fucked me, the time for gentle kisses was gone. His grip on my thighs tightened as he slammed into me, and I felt like I was going to come out of my skin when he forced one of my legs toward the wall.

I was completely open to him and he knew it. He used his hands on my thighs to hold me in place as he looked down and watched what he was doing. My legs were shaking and the urge to close them was overwhelming, but he was having none of it. He pushed them wider, impossibly so, and I shocked at the way he moved against me.

Every time his body hit mine, a shockwave ran through my clit, and I knew I wouldn't last. Liam was too good, at pleasing me, at confusing me, at making me want things I couldn't have.

"Oh, God." I clung to his shoulders and buried my face in his neck as my orgasm raked through my body.

I felt flooded by everything he was, everywhere he was touching me. It was too much. Too intense. My body fell apart and my emotions went with it.

I didn't let go of him as he thrust into me until his body fell over the edge with me or as he walked us over to his bed. I didn't let go as he laid down with me still attached to him or when he whispered my name.

I held on to him long into the night, and I didn't let the first tear fall until the rhythm of his chest slowed and his arms loosened around me.

CHAPTER 17
LIAM

I had no idea what I was doing.

How was I just supposed to go back home today and pretend like nothing had happened?

I wasn't Brooke. I couldn't just turn it on and off.

When I got up this morning, she was already packing her bag and she smiled at me like nothing had happened before. She smiled at me like she wasn't fazed at all.

But I was. I was so fucked up inside that I didn't know what to do.

I couldn't stand that shitty smile on her face or the way she told me she'd be down after she took a shower like going back home was the best thing she could imagine.

"What's wrong?" My mom was staring at me over her coffee cup, and regardless of how hard I tried to hide it, I knew I was doing a piss-poor job of it.

I shook my head and stared out the window. I couldn't tell her. I couldn't let her know that I brought Brooke here, the girl that she liked so much, just to trick her. I couldn't tell her that I fell in love with her even though it wasn't in the plans.

"I think I love Brooke." I told her the only piece of honesty I could give her.

"I know." She nodded and took a sip of her coffee as if I just told her the simplest news ever.

But it wasn't simple. Nothing about Brooke was.

I faced her fully. "How could you know if I just figured it out?"

"Son, I've known ever since you walked in the door with her."

Moms were full of it. She only thought she knew everything, but she didn't. She didn't have a clue about me and Brooke.

"That's not true." I shook my head.

"Yes. It is." She looked to the stairs as if she didn't want Brooke to overhear what she had to say next. "I don't know what you two have going on between you, but I know you haven't figured it out. Brooke looks at you like you hung the moon and she has since the moment you dropped her off in my kitchen to make biscuits."

I couldn't take it anymore. I couldn't keep lying to her.

"She was faking."

My mom shook her head, but she didn't understand.

"I'm not lying to you, Mom, she was faking this entire time. I brought her here to lie to you."

She took another sip of her coffee and stared at me as only a mama could. "Katie told me."

What? I couldn't believe her. After everything she's done, did she actually believe that telling my mom about me and Brooke was going to change anything? Did it actually change anything?

"It doesn't matter though. Whatever reason you brought that girl here, the outcome is the same. She loves you. I would much rather that be real than some two-month relationship you tried to appease me with."

"I'm sorry, Mom. I shouldn't have brought her here." I hated those words. I would never take back the decision that brought us to today. "It was wrong to lie to you, but you're wrong about her."

"I'm sorry I made you feel the need to lie. I shouldn't have put that kind of pressure on you, and I'm sorry I called you an idiot."

"You didn't." I shook my head.

"Oh, I did." She smirked. "I just said it to your dad. He thinks you're being one too."

I didn't know what to say to that.

"Don't look so shocked." She pointed at the ceiling. "That girl's in love with you and you're just going to sit here and act like it's not even happening."

"She doesn't want this."

"Then make her want it." She rolled her eyes as if I was being completely clueless.

"Okay. I think that's everything." Brooke was climbing down the stairs, and she still had that damn smile on her face. But her eyes told a different story. She looked like she was as thrilled to be going back home as I was.

"Oh." My mom rose from her chair and pulled Brooke into her arms. I winced because I didn't know what she was going to say. I didn't know if I wanted Brooke to find out that she knew the truth. Part of me would be relieved if she did, but the other part of me didn't want to give her any reason to back out of our deal.

As of right now, I still owed her, and I wanted to make

sure I didn't give her any reason to back out. I didn't want to give her any reason to run away from me.

"I wish you didn't have to go."

"Me too." My mom and Brooke were hugging each other so tightly that I wasn't sure how they were breathing. I was pretty sure that the two of them would miss each other far more than either would miss me.

"You all off already?" My dad came in from the back yard and wiped some grease off his hands. There was no telling what he had already been doing this morning.

"We are. Brooke has to be back at work tomorrow." Which she needed to quit. The building was ours, and I couldn't wait until she told that place where to shove it.

My mom and Brooke were saying something to one another that only the two of them could hear before they let each other go. My mom tucked some hair behind Brooke's ear and smiled at her. "We'll be up for a visit soon, but don't forget to text me."

"I won't." Brooke smiled sadly at her, and I hated that our deal did this to her. I didn't mean for her to come here and fall for my mama or my mama fall for her.

But I would do anything to give this to her. I would share my mama and this old house and anything else she wanted. All she had to do was say the word.

I grabbed her luggage and rolled it to the door. My dad clapped me on the back before pulling me into a hug. "Don't be a stranger."

"I won't." I moved to my mom as my dad hugged Brooke.

"And don't be an idiot." My mom's voice was soft but stern as I hugged her tiny body.

They were the only words I could think about as we

walked out of the door and got in the car, and they were the only thing I could think about as Brooke smiled at me before looking out the window.

I had been an idiot about this whole damn thing, and I didn't know what to do to make it right.

CHAPTER 18
BROOKE

We had been home for two days, and they had been two of the suckiest days of my life.

Not only had I not slept well since I had gotten used to sleeping with Liam all week, but work had been kicking my ass. Apparently taking a week off was one of the worst decisions I ever had, and I was currently making up for it.

I just kept repeating over and over in my head that things would be different soon. Liam told me that they had accepted his offer, but we hadn't discussed many details after that. I had been too busy working out the details of his body to be worried about our future.

The only positive was that I was going to see Kennedy within the next ten minutes, and I couldn't freaking wait. Of course, she wanted to have dinner at Tucker and Liam's restaurant, Rock Bottom, but it wasn't like I could tell her no.

I always loved going there before, and I should have had no reason not to go there now. But I did.

I hadn't seen Liam since he helped me carry my luggage into my apartment. I knew he was probably just as busy as I was, probably much more so, but I would be lying if I said it didn't hurt.

I pushed him away and I had no right, but I still wanted him. I wanted him to tell me I was an idiot and that I was making a stupid decision. But he was smarter than that.

I walked into Rock Bottom and immediately saw Kennedy sitting at the bar. I walked up behind her, wrapping my arms around her, and she squealed as she looked over at her shoulder at me.

"Never leave me again." She was so serious as she said it, but I couldn't help but laugh.

"Never."

I climbed onto the barstool next to her, and I waved at Chloe who was serving someone at the other end of the bar.

"I'm so freaking glad you're home." She took a sip of the soda that sat in front of her. "I need all the details."

A bartender I didn't recognize stood in front of me, and I quickly ordered a vodka soda.

"There aren't really any details." I looked around the restaurant, but I didn't see Liam or Tucker.

"Says the vodka soda." She was staring at me like she was dying for me to spill the tea.

I rolled my eyes at her. "It's been a long day."

"Sure." She took another drink. "Tucker said Liam's been extra moody since you all have been home."

"What's that got to do with me?" He hadn't been extra moody when I left him. Sure, we had barely spoken the entire car ride home, but things were weird.

"Oh. I don't know. You two have had so much sexual tension that it makes everyone around you a little hot and you've just spent a week alone together in fake love."

"Whatever." I took a long sip of my drink just as Chloe made her way over to us.

"Couldn't you have at least gave Liam a blowy while you all were gone? He's already getting on my damn nerves."

I almost spit out my drink. "Really, Chloe?"

"Oh my God. You did?" She stopped wiping down the bar and looked at me with pure delight on her face.

"No. I didn't." I answered quickly. Too quickly. It even sounded like a lie to me.

"You're lying." Kennedy pointed at me, and she looked as tickled as Chloe. "I can always tell when you're lying."

I didn't want to lie to her again, but I also didn't want either of them to make a big deal out of it. Because it wasn't a big deal. What happened, happened and that was the end of it. We didn't need to hash out all the naughty details.

Or any of the other details for that mattered.

"It isn't important." I tried to wave them off, but they weren't having any of it.

"Isn't important?" Kennedy looked at Chloe before looking at me. "You always give me the deets and now that it's with Liam fucking Gentry, you're going to hold out on me?"

"Will you please keep your voice down?" I looked behind us, but there still wasn't a sign of him.

"He's here." Chloe nodded toward the back of the restaurant. "In his office, if you want me to get him."

"No." I put my hand on top of hers to stop her.

She and Kennedy both looked up at me.

"Oh shit. You caught feelings." Chloe said it like it was the worst possible outcome.

"No. That's not it." I shook my head, but we all three knew I was lying.

They always knew when I was lying.

"Why didn't you tell me?" Kennedy was serious now, but this wasn't happening. Not here. Not now. Not where Liam could walk out at any moment.

"Can we not do this here?" I looked around the beautiful bar. "We'll talk about it later."

As soon as the words left my mouth, Liam stormed through the door to the bar and he looked pissed. He had a clipboard in his hand and the couple bartenders behind the bar gave him a wide berth as he opened one of the bottom cabinets and started rummaging through it.

"Speaking of the devil," Chloe said only loud enough for us to hear, but I still picked up my glass and chugged the rest of the vodka.

I wasn't prepared to see him. He looked as handsome as ever, but there was something about him that seemed different. It was as if there were two different Liams and this was the one I barely knew. This was the one who had known where to draw the line between us.

"Can I get another one of these?" I handed my glass to Chloe.

"Of course. Jerry, can you make Brooke another vodka soda?" She said it loud enough for the whole damn restaurant to hear, and even though we were friends, I wanted to climb across the bar and wring her neck.

She knew exactly what she was doing, and it worked. Liam looked up as soon as she said my name, and it only took a moment before his eyes landed on me.

I held my breath as he straightened and set his clipboard on the bar. He looked as if he was contemplating whether or not to come over to where we sat, and I didn't blame him.

But he made his way over to us with a smile on his face, and he leaned on his elbows on the bar right in front of Kennedy. "Well, if it isn't my favorite Mrs. Did you miss me?"

"Of course." She reached out and patted his cheek. "But I missed her more."

He looked up at me and the smile he gave me made my stomach turn. It was so fake and forced and nothing like the smiles he gave me when we were in Tennessee.

"I returned her in one piece." He said it so matter of factly but he was wrong.

I felt like I was in a million little pieces, and I didn't know how to put those pieces back together. Whatever Liam had done to me, I didn't know how to get back to the girl I was before him. Before we screwed everything up.

"I'm just happy she's home. Did you all have fun?"

"We did." He nodded. "Well, I did. I don't know about Brooke."

"I did." My answer was instant.

"Did you have everyone fooled?" Chloe set another drink down in front of me.

"I think we did a pretty fantastic job of that." He pushed is hair back out of his face, and he looked as uncomfortable as I felt.

"Mr. Gentry," the hostess interrupted us, and she looked nervous. Apparently he had been in a bad mood. "I'm sorry but your party is here for your reservation."

He looked past her to the front of the restaurant and all three of us followed his gaze to the pretty brunette in a pencil skirt and a blazer.

I had no right, but jealousy still overwhelmed me. It didn't matter what we were or weren't, my heart apparently wasn't keeping up, and I hated how instant and severe the feeling was.

"If you ladies will excuse me, I've got a quick meeting scheduled." He looked over at me, and me only. "It was good to see you."

It was good to see me? Good to see me?

Did he really just say it was good to see me? I wanted to jump over the damn bar and pound my fists into his chest. He was about to have dinner with some woman while I wasn't even sleeping and all he has to say to me is it was good to see me?

I was irrational. I knew that, but that didn't make it any better. I knew that I was the one who told him we were a bad idea, but he had instilled that idea in my head.

He had given me every reason in the world why we wouldn't be good together, and I had finally believed him. But now? Now, I wanted to take it all back.

I wanted to lay claim on him right here in front of everyone, especially that damn woman he just hugged and motioned to sit at his table.

"Down, tiger."

My gaze snapped up to Chloe.

"What?"

"You look like you're about to attack someone." She nudged my vodka soda closer to me. "That's his lawyer."

"What?" It was apparently the only word I could think of.

"She's married and has a few kids. I've been to plenty of meetings with her about the restaurant. Stop planning her death."

I looked back over at them, and sure enough, she had

pulled a file out of her bag and had paperwork laid out on the table.

"I wasn't planning her death."

"You totally were." Kennedy laughed. "But I was plotting it for you too."

"He can have dinner with whoever he wants." I was still being petty even though Chloe had just told me who she was.

"You're cute when you're jealous. It's a good look for you." I narrowed my eyes at Chloe, but she didn't care. I didn't think that girl was scared of anything.

"So, you definitely caught feelings." Kennedy wasn't asking me. She just stated the facts.

"It doesn't matter." I looked over my shoulder at him again, and this time he was looking back at me. I couldn't tell what he was thinking, I never could, but I was dying to know. I would give anything to know what was running through his mind.

"Why wouldn't it matter?" Kennedy sounded completely perplexed.

"We already decided that it wasn't a good idea. We're about to start working together and it's just not a good idea." I turned back toward them, and they were both looking at me like I was a complete idiot.

"Why can't you work together and be together? You're both professionals." Chloe was actually serious.

"Right? Like when I professionally fucked him at his mama's house during our fake relationship?"

"I knew it." Chloe held her hand out in Kennedy's direction, and Kennedy huffed before pulling a hundred dollar bill out of her pocket.

"What the hell was that?" I pointed to the money as she put it in Chloe's hand.

"Just a little bet." Chloe smiled like she had just hit the laundry. "Don't let your husband forget that he owes me too."

"You all bet on me?" These bitches. They were supposed to be my best friends and here they were placing bets on whether or not I could keep it in my pants.

"Technically, we bet on Liam. Chloe said that he couldn't resist you, but I just didn't see it coming. I didn't think you were really into him."

"That's because I'm not." The lies were just rolling off my tongue.

"Let me get you another drink while you keep lying to yourself. I've got a couple extra hundred to burn through." Chloe fanned her face with the hundred and I wanted to kill them both.

CHAPTER 19
LIAM

Brooke had left before I got a chance to talk to her. I hadn't been intentionally avoiding her, but I was swamped after missing so much work and I didn't even know where to start.

I could hear her in her apartment at night, and I wanted nothing more than to go over there and climb into her bed. I wasn't sleeping well, everyone at work was pissing me off, and I was just in a piss-poor mood overall.

And it was her fault.

Everything about this was.

Before her, everything was fine, but she flipped everything on its head.

I knocked on her door even though it was nearly ten o'clock. The meeting with my lawyer tonight was to go over some things with the purchase of the Marshall building.

But I had seen the way she looked at her.

That wasn't a girl who thought we were a bad idea. She looked like a girl who was about to lay her claim, and I would have welcomed it.

"Hey." She was in her pajamas, and she looked sleepy.

"I'm sorry. Were you asleep?" Shit. Maybe it was too late to come by.

"No." She shook her head. "I was just watching a movie. Come in."

She opened the door and I stepped into her dark apartment. There was nothing on but the TV, and I smiled as I looked down at her tiny shorts and thick wool socks.

I stood in her living room awkwardly, and she looked like she was feeling as awkward as I was.

"I brought this over." I held out the paperwork my lawyer and I had just signed, and Brooke took them from my hand.

She clicked on a lamp, drowning the room in soft light, and sat down on the edge of the couch. She looked over the papers before she looked up at me with a soft laugh. "I don't know what any of this means."

I took a deep breath and searched her eyes. I had no idea how she was going to take this. I didn't have a clue how she would react.

I pushed up my shirt sleeve and sat down beside her. My thigh touched hers and that one simple touch was like a shock to my system. I missed touching her. Even if it was fake, I missed being able to kiss her any time I wanted.

I looked at the paper in her hand and pointed to our names. "Well, this right here is showing that the property has been transferred from my name to yours."

"What?" She was searching the paper as if staring at it would somehow make her see it more clearly. "What does that mean?"

"It means that the Marshall building is yours."

She looked up at me then with no expression on her face.

I didn't know what was about to happen. I didn't have a clue as to what she was thinking.

"What do you mean it's mine?" She shook her head. "You bought the building. You said I'd be responsible for everything else."

"I know." My lawyer had told me this was a horrible decision, but this was one thing that I didn't give a shit about her opinion on. I had made up my mind on the drive home from Tennessee. I knew what I was going to do whether Brooke liked it or not. "And that's still the case. But the building is yours now."

She looked back down at the papers then back up at me. "Why are you doing this?" Her voice broke, and I hated it.

"Because you've worked your ass off. I'd still love to be in business with you, but I don't want you to think that I can hold that building over your head. The building is yours no matter what happens."

She stood from the couch and paced in front of her coffee table. She was reading the papers, really reading them, and I sat quietly on the couch while she did. I knew there was a strong likelihood this decision would piss her off, but it was an easy decision to make.

If the building was mine, Brooke would always think she owed me something, and she didn't. No matter where we went from here, she didn't owe me a thing.

"I can't accept this." She held the papers out to me as if I could just take it back.

"It's already done. I've already signed everything."

"No." She shook her head and wiped at a tear that fell down her cheek.

"Don't cry." I stood up and took a step toward her. "I didn't mean to make you cry."

"What did you think this would do?" She shook the papers at me.

"I don't know." I shrugged and moved even closer to her. "I thought you'd be happy. I thought you'd be relieved."

She threw the papers down on the table and ran her fingers through her hair. "I didn't ask you to buy me a building. I didn't want this."

"What do you want then, Brooke? Just tell me what to do."

"I want you to treat me like you would treat any other business partner. Is this how you'd treat Tucker?"

"No."

She threw her hands up at my answer, but I wasn't through.

"But I don't love Tucker."

She stopped her pacing then and she stared at me. "You don't love me." Her voice sounded so small and nothing like the girl I loved.

"Don't tell me what I feel. Regardless of what you feel, I love you."

She took a step back as I stepped forward. "We had a great week, Liam, but you're confused. Your mom and your dad..."

"Know everything."

Her head snapped up.

"Katie told them the truth before we left. Apparently she overheard you and Sophie talking about it at the football game."

Her hand slid to her neck. "Your mom."

"She's just as in love with you as she was when she thought you were my girlfriend." I wasn't lying. My mom had been blowing me up nonstop to find out if I had fixed this yet. I was pretty sure she was going to disown me if I didn't.

"What did your lawyer say about this?" She pointed to the discarded papers.

"She told me it was a horrible idea, but apparently I love horrible ideas."

She was shaking her head, but I didn't know what she wanted from me. I didn't know what she wanted me to say.

"What do you want, Brooke? If you want the building, it's yours. If you don't want the building, I'll take it back. Just tell me what you want." I sounded as desperate as I felt.

"I can't. I don't." I knew she hated the next words that came out of her mouth. It was written all over her face. "I don't want to depend on you. I don't want to depend on you and you to change your mind about me."

I didn't let her keep her distance. I closed the space with a few steps, and I buried my hands in her hair. She tried to look away from me, but I refused to let her. "I will never change my mind about you."

"You don't know that," she whispered, but she was wrong.

"Yes. I do." I kissed her forehead then pulled away slowly. "You're all that I think about. You're all I see. I couldn't change my mind about you if I tried."

She reached her hand up and gripped my hand with hers. "Promise me."

"I promise." I pressed my forehead to hers. "I love you, Brooke."

"I love you too."

I picked her up and slammed my mouth against hers. I couldn't take another second without tasting her. I wanted to know what those words felt like coming off her lips. "Say it again."

"I love you."

I fell against the couch, and she held on as she settled into my lap. I couldn't stop touching her. Kissing her.

I never wanted to stop ever again.

She reached between us and jerked her shirt over her head in an instant.

"I love your body." I ran my tongue over her nipple before running my nose along her breastbone. "I love your tits."

She laughed and ran her fingers through my hair.

"I love your lips." I kissed her as she laughed again, and I swear it was my favorite kind of kiss. I had never seen anyone as beautiful as Brooke when she laughed.

"Is there anything about me you don't love?" she teased as she started grinding against my lap.

"No." I shook my head and kissed her shoulder. "I especially love it when you do that."

She laughed and moved harder against me as she started fumbling with the buttons of my shirt. I didn't stop her. I reached down and unbuckled my belt before opening my slacks.

I had no idea how I had survived so long without her before, but right then, I felt like I was going to die if I didn't touch every inch of her.

She lifted to her knees as I pulled my cock from my pants and she slipped her shorts to the side before sitting back down against me. She rubbed her wetness against me slowly causing us both to groan before she lifted again and lined herself up with me.

I kissed up her neck as she slowly settled against me

taking me into her fully, and I had to stop myself from lifting her up and slamming her back against the couch.

I knew she needed this bit of control, and I would give it to her. Especially now. Especially after her telling me she loved me.

Her fingers dug into my shoulders as she lifted and dropped against me. The way her body moved was sinful, and I couldn't do anything but lean my head back against the couch and watch her.

Whoever had made her ever feel like she wasn't good enough had never really seen her. If they had, there would never had been a doubt in their mind.

This girl was pure fucking magic, and I was a fool for not seeing that before.

I reached into her shorts, finding her clit, and I rubbed circles to match her pace. She bit her lip as her eyes became heavy, and I wrapped my spare arm around her hips to force her closer to me.

I thrust into her as she fell back against me. I could feel her body tightening, and I was thankful because I didn't know how much longer I would last.

Being with her was unlike anything I had ever felt with anyone else. Her body was so in tune with mine. Her mouth felt like it was made for me.

She gave just as good as she got, and she was never shy about letting me know what she loved. I didn't think she could hide it if she tried.

"Liam." My name sounded like a prayer on her lips, and I wanted to give her everything.

Whatever she wanted, whatever she needed, I would give it to her.

Her thighs locked against mine, and I slammed up into

her as she fell apart above me. I felt like my hands were bruising her skin, but I couldn't stop. I wanted her closer, I wanted more, and I was never willing to let go.

"I love you, Liam," she whispered, and there wasn't a chance in hell that I wasn't following her over that edge.

I buried myself in her and bruised my lips against hers. I couldn't get enough, every touch only fueling my addiction.

But she was an addiction I would happily fall to my knees for.

"I love you." I came inside her, harder than I had ever come before, and exhaustion hit me as she laid against my chest but I wasn't done with her.

I would fall again and again, and I would never get enough.

CHAPTER 20
BROOKE

I could hear someone at the door, but I didn't care. The couch was against my back, and Liam's warm chest was against mine.

A very smooth chest, a very naked chest. I ran my fingers down his side to an also very naked hip. He let out a soft, sleepy groan and pulled me in tighter to him. Everywhere he touched, I could feel his skin.

"Wake up, sleepyhead." I registered Kennedy's voice about the same moment it clicked in my mind that we were each wrapped around each other completely naked. I reached for the blanket that was tangled at our feet, but it was too late. "Oh my God. Tucker, close your eyes."

She slammed her hand down over Tucker's eyes as she turned away from us, and I noted the large paper bag in Tucker's hand.

"What are you doing here?" I quickly covered myself and Liam as he sat up with a chuckle.

"What am I doing here?" Kennedy shrieked. "What is he doing here? I thought my best friend was going to be all depressed and mopey this morning, so I brought you your favorite French toast from that café down the street, but apparently it's not needed."

I couldn't stop smiling because she was such a good friend.

"Oh. It's needed." Liam tugged me harder into his side and nuzzled my neck. "We need fuel after last night."

"Oh my God." Kennedy peeked over her shoulder at us, and once she realized we were covered, she finally dropped her hand from Tucker's face.

Liam's hand was still holding my side, and he was rubbing his thumb over my bare skin. It made me want to jump him and feel panicky all at the same time.

I couldn't believe he was here and that he loved me. I couldn't believe that all of this was real.

Tucker set the bag down on the coffee table in front of us as Kennedy paced.

"So, what happened here?" She pointed between the two of us.

"Well, first I took off my shirt then…"

"That's not what I mean and you know it. Is this a fling or?"

"It's not a fling." Liam's answer was instant.

She put her hands on her hips as she studied him. "Then what are your intentions with my best friend?"

I couldn't stop my small snort at how ridiculous she was being, but I also loved her for it. She was all I had, and she took that position very seriously.

"I intend to be naked with her a lot, so I would suggest you start knocking."

Tucker chuckled, but Kennedy didn't look nearly as pleased.

"And do you plan to date her while the two of you are getting naked?"

"Well, I love her, so I would say so."

Hearing him say those words again felt unreal. Everything about this did.

Kennedy's face immediately morphed into the biggest damn grin. "You love her?"

Okay. She was starting to embarrass me now. The way she said it was like she didn't know her girl would ever find it.

"I do." He, on the other hand, sounded like he had never been more sure of anything in his life.

"Oh my God." She looked over at Tucker before grabbing his hands. "We should go. They clearly need some time alone."

"You don't have to leave." Liam pinched me as I said it. Apparently, he was more than happy for them to give us some alone time.

Tucker pulled his keys from his pocket and dangled them in the air. "We could go defile Liam's apartment for old time's sake." He nuzzled Kennedy's neck as she laughed.

"Deal."

They walked to the door as Liam huffed. "You all have your own damn house now. Go there."

"It's not as exciting." Kennedy opened the door and pointed at the bag on the table. "I hope you enjoy my breakfast, Liam, but take your time." She winked and we could hear them giggling out in the hallway.

"They're going to destroy your apartment." I couldn't help laughing as I started pulling all sorts of delicious treats from the bag. Kennedy really did expect me to be depressed and moping.

"I don't think they left a surface untouched before they moved out. I'm not too worried about it."

I poured a small container of syrup over my French toast as I thought about my once prude best friend. "You might want to hire a cleaning service because Kennedy's turning into quite the little freak."

He laughed and dipped his finger into my syrup.

"Hey," I said just as he ran that same finger over my bare shoulder.

Sticky syrup covered my skin, and I couldn't look away as he used his tongue to clean it off me.

"I'm a little more concerned with making sure you're clean." He dipped his finger in the syrup again and a few drops fell on my blanket before he dripped it down my chest.

"This is going to be a mess." I wasn't just talking about the syrup.

"Yeah." He jerked my legs toward him and my back hit the couch. He got to his knees and leaned over me, and he watched the syrup as it ran toward my neck. "But you're going to love it."

He was right. I was going to love every second of it.

EPILOGUE
BROOKE

I couldn't believe this was actually happening.

Everything had happened so fast, and I couldn't believe that it was finally here.

I took a sip from my champagne flute, trying to shake off my nerves, and I looked around my business.

My business.

More Than Enough Salon and Spa had been an absolute labor of love over the last year. But every busy day and excruciatingly long night was worth it.

Liam had been my biggest supporter and had spent almost an equal amount of long nights helping me make it what it has become, but every single inch of this place was me. They were my decisions, my choices, and Liam never made me feel like they weren't enough.

It was the opposite really. He encouraged everything I did, and despite what I had ever thought about him, Liam had become the best hype man I could have ever asked for.

Besides Kennedy, I had never had that in my life.

She was currently getting a manicure, and I couldn't stop

smiling at the way she was asking the nail tech to make them shorter for the third time since she started.

The spa was staffed with a receptionist, three cosmetologist, two nail techs, two estheticians, and three massage therapists, and they were all ready with smiles on their faces.

None of this would have been possible without Liam.

True to his word, he put the building in my name and I purchased everything else. Our profits would be split fifty/fifty, and if they didn't come in soon, I would be moving in with Kennedy and Tucker.

Paying for the everything else took every last penny I had, and it didn't matter that Liam had offered to help me more. I wouldn't have it. He had helped enough, and I needed to do the rest on my own. I needed to prove to myself that I could do this.

"Can you believe this?" I was standing at the receptionist desk admiring everything when Liam walked up behind me and pressed a kiss to my shoulder.

I took a deep breath because I honestly wasn't sure. The siding was painted the perfect shade of white, the flowers lining the walkway the perfect shade of purple, and every single thing on the inside was exactly how I imagined, but none of that would have mattered if today wasn't successful.

"No." I shook my head as looked out at the packed grand opening.

"You're amazing." He pressed another gentle kiss before placing his hands on my hips and turning me toward him. "I knew today would be incredible."

I wrapped my arms around his shoulders and let him bare some of the weight I had been carrying around for the last week. I had never been so stressed out in my life. "You have too much faith in me."

His hair was still perfectly in place as it always was, but his facial hair had grown out a bit. There was just a slight shadow of hair on his face, but it somehow made him impossibly hotter.

"I don't." He tucked a piece of hair behind my ear. "You have too little."

I rolled my eyes because he'd said it so often.

But I was working on believing it.

"I've had too little of you lately." I ran one hand over his scruff. "I miss you."

Between the opening of my business plus him running his, it seemed like we barely had time for each other. It didn't matter that we spent every moment we weren't working with each other or that he had practically moved into my apartment. I still wanted more.

"I miss you too." He moved closer to me, his mouth at my ear. "I'll make sure you have plenty of me tonight."

"You're so cocky."

"And you love it." He kissed along my jaw, and I could almost forget where we were. That was the thing about Liam, he always made me forget everything but him. "Speaking of love, someone's here to see you."

He was looking past me, and I turned in his arms to see who he was talking about. Everyone who I had personally invited was already here.

I almost fell out of his arms when his mama's smiling face came into view.

"Oh my God." I pushed him out of my way and ran toward Sarah like I hadn't seen her in forever. It had actually only been two months, but I wasn't expecting her here today. I didn't think she was going to be able to come. "What are you doing here?"

She wrapped me in her arms, like she always did, and I fell into her like she was a home I had never found. Not until Liam.

"I wouldn't miss this for the world." Her arms tightened around me. "Jim's here too."

I looked behind her, and sure enough, there he was standing in the middle of my spa looking a bit uncomfortable and a lot proud.

"Come here, sweetheart." He pulled me away from Sarah and wrapped me up in his warmth, and I suddenly felt overwhelmed.

This whole day, these people, it was too much.

"We're so proud of you."

I buried my face in his chest and tried to gain my composure. I had so many people here supporting me, but there was something about Liam's parents that made everything feel more real. It made everything feel like I deserved everything I had worked for.

I loosened my grip on his shirt and cleared my throat as I finally let him go. "Thank you."

He was smiling down at me, and he knew I was about to lose it. "I've never been more proud of any of my son's fake girlfriend's before."

I couldn't help the small laugh that bubbled out of me, and I knew that was his intention. Jim was like that.

Sarah smacked his arm as she rolled her eyes. "Or any of his real ones."

"Let's go get you a treatment." I grabbed Sarah's hand in mine and led her toward one of my estheticians who was just following up a sample treatment on someone else.

I got her set up before making rounds throughout the rest

of the spa. I couldn't believe everything was running as smoothly as it was, but I was soaking it all in.

I hadn't been this happy in as long as I could remember, and it wasn't because of the spa. It had everything to do with Liam.

The last year with him had been amazing and challenging. Neither one of us really knew what we were doing when it came to a relationship, but both of us had been willing to try.

It turned out that I was a bit jealous, and Liam was a little too overprotective. It ended in fights too often, but the make-up sex made it worth it. He was worth it.

By the time the evening started winding down and people started to leave, my feet were tired and my chest ached from all the support I had gotten today. It far exceeded what we had expected, and it made me so hopeful for what the future held.

The girls working here were all lovely and had truly stepped up today for the grand opening. I wanted them to love working here. I never wanted them to hate their jobs like I used to.

I was wiping down the reception desk while Liam shut the front door, and when he turned back toward me with a smile on his face, I couldn't believe this was my life.

I couldn't believe that I was getting everything I had ever wanted.

"My parents are staying at my place tonight." Liam reached for my hand and I let him take it. "That means you're stuck with me at yours."

"What if I don't want to deal with you anymore tonight?"

He tugged me toward him and my chest slammed into his. "That's just too damn bad. You're stuck with me."

"How so?" I couldn't stop running my fingers over the scruff on his face.

"Well, we're business partners now."

I rolled my eyes playfully. "They usually don't sleep in each other's beds."

He completely ignored my comment. "Plus, we've graduated from fake boyfriend and girlfriend to real boyfriend and girlfriend."

"Nothing in that sentence makes me stuck with you. I can get rid of you whenever I want without much work."

He cocked his head as if he was considering what I said. "That's true. Maybe I should make it harder."

He took a small step back from me, and I had no clue what he was doing. He was grinning like today had been the best day of his life when it reality it had been the best day of mine, and he had made it that way.

"What are you doing?"

He was only one step away from me when he gripped his slacks just at his thighs and shifted them up as he bent to his knee. I looked down to see if one of his shoes were untied or maybe there was a scuff mark on the floor. Anything that would give a logical explanation for why this man would be kneeling in front of me right now.

"Brooke, I know this relationship of ours started off a little unconventionally, but I wouldn't take one moment of it back. I knew I loved you when we were still faking it, and I've known it every day since." He shifted his hands in front of him, and I held my breath as I watched him. "Our first relationship agreement had come with a deal, and I think that this one should to." He held a delicate intricate ring in front of him, and I stared down at it without a word. I could barely manage a small breath. "If you'll agree to marry me, I promise to do everything in my power to make you happy. I'll try to not be so overprotective, and I'll never complain about the amount of shoes you buy."

I could feel tears filling my eyes and I tried to blink them away as I responded. "It would seem I'm getting the better end of this deal."

He shook his head quickly as if it was the most absurd thing I had ever said. "Trust me, baby girl. I am."

He was still on his knee, and I couldn't believe this was happening. I looked around us at everything we had already accomplished together, but none of it would have mattered. None of it mattered except him.

"Yes. Of course, I'll marry you." I reached out toward the ring, but he pulled it away.

"I think we should set some ground rules first."

I couldn't help but laugh. "And what would those be?"

"There will definitely be kissing and lots of sex."

I rolled my eyes and took a small step closer to him. "Anything else?"

"Yea." He nodded as he stood and gripped my hand in his. I watched as he slipped the ring onto my finger, and I had the weirdest feeling that I had seen that ring before. "You have to promise to never leave me."

I looked up at him and wrapped my hands around his neck. My left hand suddenly heavier in the most delicious way. "I promise."

He kissed me then, a kiss that I would remember for the rest of my life, and I fell into him as I always had. He made it impossible to do anything less.

"I love you." He kissed my lips then my jaw then my nose.

"I love you too."

"Are you happy?" He whispered his question against my skin.

"I've never been happier in my life."

He smiled and gripped my hand in his. We both looked down at it, his ring fitting perfectly on my finger.

"Liam?"

"Yea?"

I was still staring down at the somehow familiar ring. "Where did you get this ring?"

His smile seemed to double at my question. "It was my mama's." He lifted my hand and pressed a kiss against my ring. "My dad proposed to her with it thirty-five years ago, and she wanted you to have it."

I took a deep breath and tried to calm down my racing heart. "It's too much." I shook my head. A girl like me didn't get everything. I couldn't have everything I had ever dared dream of.

"No." He gripped my face in his hands and stared down at me like a man who was completely and irrevocably in love. "It's perfect."

And for the first time in my life, I believed him.

DIDN'T GET ENOUGH?

**You've fallen for the trouble.
Now it's time to meet the cowboys who'll ruin
you for anyone else.**

If you like your romance dirty-mouthed, slow-burn, high heat, and downright addictive, you'll want to head straight to the Calloway Ranch.

Keep Reading for a sneak peek of
Cowboy Casual!

CHAPTER 1
BLAIRE

The photos landed in my inbox at 5:37 p.m. Another email, this one with the subject line URGENT: For Review- Grant Chandler Jr.

I barely blinked. Just another Thursday at Senator Monroe's office, where my job as press assistant meant I spent half my time putting out fires before they spread all over the internet. A few clicks, some carefully crafted lies, and by dinner, the world would be slightly less on fire and my father's re-election chances marginally more secure.

I spent four years at Duke getting my marketing degree, and here I was, a glorified janitor for my father's indiscretions and political messes. My professors would be proud to see that their star pupil's primary skill set had become making scandals disappear before they hit the trending page.

But the name at the top of the email wasn't my father's. It was my fiancé's.

The Chandlers had been bankrolling my father's campaigns since before I came to live with him, their hedge fund fortune buying the influence that kept both families comfortable. Four years ago, my father seated me next to Grant at a fundraiser. I was finishing my last year at Duke, and my father's eyes gleamed with approval every time Grant leaned in to whisper something that made me laugh.

Two hours and three glasses of merlot later, I'd mistaken his calculated attention for charm, and the next morning, roses crowded my tiny apartment doorway with a note that simply read, "Dinner? -Grant."

That one yes led to a diamond ring that had been on my finger for the last fourteen months, and now the wedding was a little over a hundred days away.

I opened the email, and the images loaded one by one. I noticed Grant first, then his assistant, who was splayed across his mahogany desk. Her blouse was unbuttoned, and his fingers tangled in her dark hair while the other hand gripped her skirt, wrinkling the expensive fabric I'd complemented her on last month. There was a hunger in his eyes I'd never seen in our bedroom.

More images followed as I scrolled, each one a blow. My stomach clenched. There they were in a D.C. hotel elevator, and the timestamp mocked me. Taken exactly fifteen days after the engagement party my father had thrown for us. Another showed them at some dimly lit bar. Grant wore a navy suit with a pale blue tie I'd tied for him the morning of his keynote speech. She draped her thigh across him, and his hand disappeared beneath the hem of her dress.

I scrolled through the evidence of his betrayal. In some, they were alone. In others, they exchanged secretive touches at campaign events where I stood just yards away, smiling for donors while his fingers found her waist.

The first photo was from thirteen months ago, and the most recent was from yesterday afternoon.

My vision blurred as I stared at the photos. A laugh from the bullpen made me flinch, and my gaze landed on the framed picture on my desk. Grant and I were at the Children's Hospital benefit. Grant's hand gripped my hip, his fingers digging in enough to remind me to stand straighter for the cameras. I'd wanted to wear the black dress I'd picked out myself, but he'd replaced it with the lavender gown that was hanging in our closet when I returned from work. "Trust me," he'd said, his voice firm.

I waited for the rage, for the tears, but found neither. Instead, my fingers shook against the keyboard as the room tilted and narrowed around me. In that moment, I felt the snap of that invisible thread that bound me to this life, to my father's ambitions and Grant's possessive hands.

In its absence came the rush, the flood, the name I'd locked away years ago.

Colt.

I physically recoiled from my own thoughts. *No. Not now. Not him.* I'd buried him beneath years of careful compartmentalization, sealed him away in the darkest corner of my heart where dangerous things belonged. He'd gutted me in ways Grant's betrayal couldn't touch, yet here he was, the first name my mind reached for.

The contradiction made me sick. Hating him and the physical ache of wanting him after all these years. I feared what that meant about who I really was beneath all these perfect, polished lies I'd wrapped around myself like expensive armor that suddenly felt paper thin.

I stood so fast my chair clipped the wall and made the edges of my vision pulse. There was a ringing in my ears as I willed myself not to look at the humiliating photos again. Everyone in this office would see them soon enough, and I should have been doing damage control. That was my job, but I suddenly couldn't give a shit about this job.

Instead, I walked straight out into the hall, closing my office door behind me with a soft click. My heels echoed on the tile as I moved, mechanical and purposeful, each step meant to keep the panic from overtaking me.

The hallway outside my office was lined with campaign posters, and today the images of my father felt like sentries watching me, silent and expectant. I tried to draw a full breath, but the air stuck in my throat and went nowhere.

I picked up my pace, crossing the bullpen and weaving past the clutch of interns hunched over their laptops. Someone tried to get my attention, but I brushed past, offering only a brittle smile I hoped passed for apologetic. The elevator was slow as hell, so I ducked into the stairwell, grateful for the emptiness and the way the steps forced my body to move.

Three flights down, I stopped, leaning against the cool cement wall. My phone buzzed in my pocket, and I yanked it out, half expecting a message from Grant. But it was my father's assistant's name looking back at me.

Judy: Senator Monroe would like for you to meet him in his office immediately.

I stared down at the screen as if my entire future hadn't just imploded.

I should have been thinking about Grant. His betrayal. The years I'd spent smoothing his rough edges, convincing myself we were in love instead of two people playing assigned roles in someone else's strategy. I should have been furious or at least humiliated. But standing in that cold stairwell, an emptiness clawed through my chest, a ravenous, familiar void that didn't belong to Grant at all.

The realization ached inside me like a bruise pressed too hard, spreading from my sternum outward until even my fingertips felt tender with the truth I'd spent years denying. My body remembered what my brain had worked overtime to forget. His thumb tracing the freckles across my collarbone, the lake water dripping from his eyelashes as he surfaced beside me, the way my name sounded like a prayer when he whispered it against my neck at dawn. I hated how easily these memories returned, how they still burned beneath my skin while Grant's betrayal felt like nothing more than a paper cut.

I despised myself for it, for looking at evidence of my fiancé's infidelity and feeling only relief tangled with shame. The pain of losing Colt had carved hollows inside me I'd filled with pretty lies and my father's approval.

I started to turn back toward my father's office, because that's what the text demanded and that's what a dutiful daughter would do. But my body revolted. My hand hovered above the banister, knuckles white against the chipped paint, and I looked up the stairwell, concrete spiraling overhead.

Then my gaze dropped, my ears ringing, and saw an exit sign pulsing red at the base of the stairs like a dare. I pressed downward, footsteps echoing against the steps, and the farther I got from the office, the easier it was to breathe. My body was moving faster than my thoughts, and that felt like freedom.

By the time I hit the last step, my legs were numb. I didn't hesitate at the landing, didn't even process what I'd do next. Instead, I barreled toward the side exit, shoved open the steel door, and found myself in the narrow alley between the Monroe Senate offices and the looming black glass of Chandler & Chandler.

The sun hung low between the tall buildings, gilding the edges of everything it touched and forcing me to shield my eyes. When the door slammed behind me, I tried to breathe as my reflection fractured across the dark, mirrored windows of Grant's building. Three days ago, I'd walked through those same doors with his favorite sandwich and a smile, playing the role of the doting fiancée for an audience of receptionists.

I should've stopped to think and called my father. I should've done what I'd been trained to do. But all I could see was Grant's hand on another woman's thigh, and the way his smile had always held a flicker of calculation. For four years, I'd filed myself down, smoothed away any parts of me that might snag on propriety or expectation. Now something untamed and forgotten stirred beneath my ribs, screaming for me to be reckless, even as my father's voice in my head listed all the ways this would destroy everything I'd worked for.

I could feel myself being torn between the wild-hearted girl my mom had raised me to be and the dull woman my father had created.

Grant's building was emptying for the evening. Men and women in tailored suits filtered out the revolving doors, but I didn't slow down. I ignored the polite smiles offered by familiar faces. A few gazes caught on me, lingering a bit too long, and my skin prickled beneath their stares. The knowing glances made my stomach twist. Had they all seen the photos already? Or worse, had they watched Grant and his assistant slip in and out of his office for months while I'd been the oblivious fiancée?

I flattened my shaking hands against my skirt, smoothing wrinkles that had set in like permanent creases. My cheeks burned with each heartbeat, a flush I couldn't hide, but I lifted my chin and locked my shoulders back, marching into Grant's building before I could stop myself.

I passed the security desk, and the guard's eyes flicked up, then away. No need to check my ID when my father's face was on billboards and my fiancé's name was etched on the side of the building. I crossed to the elevator bank and jabbed my finger against the executive floor button, leaving a smudge on the polished brass.

The ride up was dizzying. Every surface in the elevator was a mirror, and three different women were reflected back at me. There was the Senator's daughter in her expensive suit and perfect posture purchased with years of correction. Then the jilted fiancé, with anger burning behind her trembling chin and firmly pressed lips where she'd learned to swallow her voice.

And then there was *her*. The one with wide eyes and color high in her cheeks, the one who looked like my mother. I wanted to scream at her, beg her to run, to fight, to do anything.

I'd let them kill her so slowly I hadn't even noticed she was dying.

The elevator groaned somewhere above me, the floor indicator ticking up, and I caught my mother's eyes in my reflection. Her dare and mischief flickered there, then disappeared beneath my father's careful mask. I touched my face, half-expecting to feel her sunlight warming my skin, but my fingers met only the sweat-damp foundation I'd applied that morning to cover my freckles.

My mother wouldn't recognize me if she saw me now, and I hated the way my mind still drifted to Colt, desperately wondering if he'd be the one person who could still see through to whatever remained of me.

What the hell was wrong with me? I should have been devastated about Grant, not feeling this treacherous relief.

The elevator jerked to a stop. I closed my eyes for a single, shaky breath, then wiped away a stray tear before it could mar my mascara. Just one tear was all I allowed myself to shed for the girl I used to be, the girl who'd been taught her worth came from men who never really loved her.

A soft chime announced my arrival as the doors parted to reveal a wall of windows framing the sunset-washed skyline. The remaining staff sat at their desks, sliding papers into briefcases and shutting down computers, their gazes carefully avoiding mine as I moved toward the frosted glass door that separated me from Grant's office.

Without knocking, I shoved open the door, and they sprang away from each other. His assistant met my gaze while her fingers straightened her shirt. Mascara tracks stained her cheeks.

Grant ran his fingers over his tie and offered his practiced smile. "Blaire, baby. What are you doing here?"

His assistant turned away, busying herself with paperwork on his desk, but I caught the way her hands shook.

I almost felt sorry for her.

"I thought we were meeting for dinner?" Grant's voice overlapped itself, the end of the sentence scraping against the beginning, like he was trying to race ahead of the silence

I'd brought into the room. He took a step around her, positioning himself directly in front of me.

"Don't act like you don't know that I've seen the photos." My voice was steady, but my hands trembled so hard I had to dig my nails into my palms to hold them still. "How long has this been going on?"

There was a twitch in his jaw, but he kept his mask perfectly in place. "Come on, don't do this here." He tried to close the space between us, palm open, but I jerked away so fast I nearly toppled a crystal award he'd won for service to his community off his bookshelf.

"Do not make a scene," he hissed, jaw clenched tight, and eyes darting to the open door behind me.

The command landed like a slap, and my heartbeat thundered in my ears as that wild-hearted Blaire clawed her way out.

"Should I whisper about you fucking your assistant, Grant?" I didn't recognize my own voice, how it carried across the room. "Would that be more convenient for you?"

His eyes darkened as his shoulders squared. "We should discuss this at home. Privately."

He reached for my elbow, but I stepped back. "No."

"Blaire." He said my name like he was speaking to a trained dog, and I recoiled.

"Don't touch me," I said, and I heard the tremor in my voice, which only made me angrier, but the look on Grant's face told me the words landed as I intended. "Nothing you say will change what you did."

"Blaire," he tried again, gentler now. "Let's take some time to think about how we want to handle this, okay? I'll call your father—"

"Of course you will," I cut in. "You're such a fucking coward, Grant."

He flinched. Not enough that anyone else would notice, but I'd spent four years learning the tells of Grant Chandler. The tic in his jaw, the flicker behind his eyes when his composure slipped. I recognized the look of a man cornered, and it thrilled and terrified me that I was the one who'd put him there.

"This is my office. People are watching," he hissed as he angled his body like he was going to shut the door. "Let's be smart about this."

"Smart," I repeated, and the laugh that escaped me was raw and humorless. "Where were your smarts when you were fucking her on your desk? Did you think no one would notice? Or did you think I wouldn't care?"

"I never meant for you to find out like this," he said calmly. "I was going to tell you. I— I needed the right time. You know how your father is. How important this is for all of us."

I could hardly breathe as I thought of my father's ambitions, my own perfectly curated life, and the unyielding gravity of "all of us." It made me want to scream.

"My father." The words clawed at my throat as my gaze fell to the ring on my finger, the weight of the diamond suddenly crushing every bone in my hand.

"Yes, your father, Blaire," he said, drawing out each word as if I were too stupid to keep up. He leaned in, dropping the mask of concern for something infinitely colder. "Don't act fucking daft. He'll get a handle on this, and we'll figure it out."

"There's nothing to figure out." I shook my head. "I can't do this."

"Where the fuck else would you go?" He laughed, and his words hit hard, harder than I'd braced for. "You live in my condo, Blaire. You work for your father, whose campaign is funded by mine. The life you live is because of me, so don't act like you're better than this."

I had grown used to Grant's cruel words, but somehow, they still sliced through me like a blade. He was right, wasn't he? My clothes hung in his closet, my career existed at my father's mercy, and even my engagement ring had been passed down through generations of Grant's family. But I had built this life too. I had sacrificed for it, shaped myself to fit in it.

The phone on his desk rang loudly, making me flinch. His assistant lunged for it, her voice a distant buzz until she thrust the receiver in my direction, her eyes wide with fear. "Ms. Monroe, it's your father."

My stomach dropped as I brushed past Grant, my fingers clumsy as they closed around the handset.

"Dad—"

"Come to my office. Now." His tone was so measured and so infuriatingly calm that rage flooded me, making my teeth clench so hard my jaw ached.

"No." The word ripped from my throat, and I shook my head even though he couldn't see me. "You don't get to ask me to swallow this. Not for you. Not for him."

"Don't be foolish, Blaire. Grant made a mistake. All men make mistakes." My father's voice slithered through the phone like poison. I locked eyes with Grant across the room, watching him watch me, and I felt like I was suffocating.

My fingers trembled against the ring, twisting it once, twice, before hesitating at the knuckle. The diamond caught the light, beautiful and cold. I yanked it off, wincing as it scraped my skin, then traced my finger over the pale indent left behind. I squeezed the metal in my palm until it bit into my flesh, drawing comfort from the pain.

"Go to hell, dad."

I hung up before I could hear my father's response, and the phone clattered into the cradle.

Grant's eyes darted between my face and the ring clenched in my fist. I thought he was about to plead, but instead, he said, "You're being childish."

I tried to move past him, but Grant moved faster. His hand shot out, catching my arm above the elbow. He held on like he thought he could will the moment backward, as if the world would reset if I stood still long enough.

The heat of his palm bled through my shirt, and I remembered every time he'd touched me gently for the camera, every time he'd squeezed my shoulder in public, always anchoring me to his side. I'd mistaken that pressure for security, but now it felt like a vise.

"You're not leaving until we talk about this." His voice dropped to a growl, low and ugly. He yanked me closer, pulling me off balance.

I twisted my arm, trying to pry him off, but his grip tightened, his thumb digging into the soft flesh inside my elbow.

"Grant," his assistant whispered his name from behind me, but he didn't acknowledge her.

"You're hurting me," I gasped, and this time, I wrenched free.

His face went slack with surprise, as if he couldn't believe I'd dare resist him.

"Never put your hands on me again," I said, my voice steadier than my heart, as the diamond's edge bit into my palm.

Ten years ago, on a night that still woke me up sweating, I'd stood in the gravel driveway of my grandmother's house and hurled Colt's necklace at his chest because I couldn't make him choose me.

But I couldn't bring myself to hurl this ring at Grant, couldn't bring myself to care enough. I opened my aching fist and let the ring fall to the ground, watching it bounce once before settling.

I thought he might grab for me again, but he just stared, mouth tight, as I stepped past him into the hall. I walked in a trance, the blood in my ears so loud I barely heard Grant call after me.

But his words chased me with a desperate, low chuckle. "You'll be back."

I forced myself to keep walking, and I didn't stop until I was jabbing my finger against the elevator button, then again, harder. I didn't want to think about what would happen if I didn't leave right now, if I let the old gravity pull me back toward the familiar controlling orbit of Grant, my father, and all the plans they'd fused around me like a glass cage.

The elevator doors finally slid open, and I stepped inside. Four years of my life stood behind me. Security, status, a future. I pressed my back against the wall and watched the doors close, avoiding looking at my reflection. My hands shook as I pulled out my phone and dialed my grandmother's number.

She answered on the third ring, her voice calm and steady as always. "Hello."

I opened my mouth, but nothing came out but a strangled sound somewhere between a gasp and a sob.

"Blaire?" Panic edged her voice, crackling through the connection. "What's wrong?"

"Can I come home?" The words tumbled out, raw and clumsy. I waited for the guilt, the flood of regret for throwing away everything I'd built, but all I felt was an overwhelming, dangerous relief that flooded through my chest like the first breath after nearly drowning.

"Always, baby." No questions, no hesitation.

I pressed the button for the ground floor. The elevator plunged downward, and with it came visions of Colt, the curve of his jaw, the calluses on his fingertips, the weight of judgment I'd find in his gaze. My lungs seized at the thought. I was going back to the place I'd fled a decade ago, back to where Colt Calloway's words had severed me from my roots, but now those same roots called me home.

CHAPTER 2
BLAIRE

One of the very first things my grandmother taught me was that men ain't shit.

I considered getting those exact words tattooed across my forehead since, somehow, I kept needing the reminder.

But I hadn't really believed her then or when she told me I'd be back home someday.

She hadn't fought me when I packed my bags at seventeen, tears in my eyes and a fire under my skin, chasing the escape only a dumb, brokenhearted girl believed in. After months of resisting, I'd finally given in to my father's demand to go live with him, and she'd watched me go, steady and sure, while muttering, "You'll find your way back when you need to."

I'd laughed then, but I wasn't laughing now. Not with the Tennessee heat pressing in through my cracked windows, thick with the smell of honeysuckle and bittersweet memories. Memories that, no matter how hard I tried to forget, always found their way back.

My knuckles ached against my grip on the steering

wheel as my car hugged each curve of the road I could have driven with my eyes closed. Willow Grove had always moved slower, softer somehow, and from the looks of it, not much had changed.

But I sure as hell had.

I drummed my fingers on the steering wheel, the weight of my whole life rattling in the back seat in two overpriced suitcases my father had gifted me as an engagement present.

It had only been a little over a week since I found out about Grant's affair, but I'd already boxed up my life and handed in my resignation. My father had told me that I was making a mistake, that I was making foolish emotional decisions because I was hurt. Maybe I was, but the anger felt cleaner and safer somehow. There had been so many times when I'd let my anger with him and with Grant dissolve into forgiveness, but I clung to it now, tight enough to make up for all the times I swallowed it down.

My mama had always said I was as stubborn as Grandma June, and that one day, it would come back to bite me. But I wished I'd held on to it tighter, so I didn't feel so lost.

Back with Mama and June, I'd never had to guess where I belonged. They'd carved out a space for me that fit just right, and the realization that I'd traded that certainty for empty promises left a gnawing pain beneath my ribs.

The urge to call June and tell her never mind clawed at me every hour of the last week. When I finally did, her, "Hello, my girl," knocked the wind clean out of me. I opened my mouth to beg her to tell me what to do, then closed it again, but June had always seen right through me anyway, straight to the parts I hid from everyone else, including myself.

She let out a breath, tired but knowing, and I pictured

her sitting in that old kitchen chair, phone cord twisted around her finger like it used to be. "Sometimes you gotta face the music, even if it ain't your favorite tune," she said, and I both resented and clung to how she made it sound like the simplest decision in the world.

Like I wasn't headed back to a town that was not only haunted with memories of my mama, but of *him*.

The urge to ask her about Colt was a relentless itch beneath my skin, but I'd clenched my teeth and willed myself into silence before the words could tumble out. Because asking would've made it real. It would've admitted that I still thought about him, that I could still feel him in the cracks I couldn't quite close, and that his voice still echoed in my mind on nights when I drank too much and let myself remember.

It had been years since I said his name out loud, years since I heard the deep rasp of his laugh or the quiet hush of his voice in the dark, but my body refused to forget.

It was impossible to abandon the memory the way we fell into one another after years of easy friendship or the way he had touched me as if he'd been starved for me his entire life. But it was how he'd pushed me away that lingered the most, the way he had told me to leave, his voice cold and final, when my father came for me.

I told myself he didn't matter anymore. That I could steel myself if our paths crossed. But ever since I'd made the call to June, I'd been bracing for him.

Bracing for the anger, for the ache, for the boy that haunted my memories, and for the man he might've become that I no longer knew.

So when the town sign passed by in a blur, my breath caught without warning.

Welcome to Willow Grove. Population: Too damn small.

Small enough everyone would know my business by morning and have an opinion on it by lunch. They'd know I was back after years of running with nothing but a busted-up heart and a canceled engagement to show for it.

And Grant wouldn't be the only reason for the whispers that would follow me. This town had a long memory. They all knew I'd been broken before I ever left, that I was already damaged goods when I accepted Grant's ring.

I didn't slow down when I hit the split in the road. Right would take me to Main Street and left would take me past the Calloway Ranch, then to my grandmother's. I flicked on my blinker and veered left.

I didn't let myself look. I kept my eyes on the road, but I already knew what was there—the weathered fence line, worn soft from years of storms and sun, the fields that seemed to never end, and the glint of the lake in the distance.

Acres of land that had been built with blood, sweat, and generations of work. Land that Colt Calloway would never leave. I tried to force myself to forget what it was like to be loved on that land, but it was impossible.

A cluster of horses grazed in the distance, their dark shapes moving slowly across the fields. My stomach knotted at the sight that was too tied to him and every summer we'd spent on horseback. The Calloways had been our neighbors for my entire life, so I knew that land as well as I once knew Colt.

June's farmhouse appeared over the next hill, hunched beneath ancient oaks and weeping willows that were bigger than I remembered, their branches almost touching the ground.

The old mailbox came into view with *Cates* still painted

on the side in June's messy handwriting, and a smile curved my lips as I pulled onto the long gravel drive.

The house hadn't changed a bit. Four rocking chairs lined the wraparound porch, though the wood was fading and the cushions flattened thin. Tangles of battered wind chimes hung from the eaves, tinkling in the breeze.

June was already waiting there, leaning against the doorframe.

She wiped her hands on the apron tied around her thin waist, and she looked exactly how I remembered. Her skin was kissed by the sun, and her gray hair was tied in two long braids with curls framing her face she couldn't quite tame.

She greeted me with a warm smile, her eyes crinkling at the corners, and waved like I'd only been gone for the afternoon. Even from my car, I could see the way she watched me with a fierce, steady gaze that was full of the strength born from years of loving deeply, enduring loss, and shaping the world around her with her bare hands.

I cut the engine and left the car door hanging open as I crossed the yard as quickly as I could. The screen door groaned with a creaky protest as she nudged it open with her hip, and I climbed the steps two at a time.

June caught me in a hug, and all at once, I was a kid again, skinny, barefoot, covered in dirt, and wrapped around her legs as she hulled strawberries.

She smelled like flour and lemons, and beneath it, a faint trace of a day spent with her hands in the dirt. I held on as long as she let me, until she pulled back, hands framing my cheeks and her eyes roaming over every inch of my face.

"There's my little strawberry." Her voice was like warm honey, but I heard the threads of worry that were stitched into her words where she thought I wouldn't notice.

Only three people ever called me that nickname, my mama, June, and Colt, and for a long time, I had hated it.

But today? It felt like coming home, and I clung to the way it fell from her lips.

"June." I sighed my grandma's name, which I'd started using when I was twelve. I still remembered the day I got my first period, and she told me I was a woman. And women, apparently, called her June. I'd felt so grown then, but I was nothing like the woman she raised me to be anymore. I placed my hands over hers and tried to take in every subtle change. "I'm twenty-eight years old. Don't you think I've outgrown that?"

Her eyes sparkled with mischief as she reached up and gently tousled my hair, now more muted auburn than the copper fire it used to be. "You're never too old to be my little strawberry."

For a moment, I let myself believe it, that I could find my way back, that I could be the girl I used to be, but then my phone vibrated in my pocket. I ignored it, rolling my eyes at my grandmother as if that vibration didn't course through every part of me until my stomach twisted. I already knew who it was without pulling my phone out of my jeans.

I wanted to ignore Raleigh and everything that came with it. But the weight of what I'd left behind tugged at me like an undertow. I'd have to face it all eventually, the broken engagement, Grant's betrayal, and my father's disappointment. Just not yet. I'd already called off the wedding and sent my resignation, but the fight would come anyway. My father and the Chandlers always turned "no" into a negotiation, but standing on June's porch, I wanted to pretend I could start over.

"If I'm old enough for Botox," I muttered, pushing my hair out of my face, "I'm too old for that nickname."

"You're still as stubborn as a mule," she said as her eyes scoured over me, and I did the same to her. The lines around her eyes were deeper, and there were new crinkles around the corners of her mouth, proof of a life well lived and well loved.

"Maybe even more so." I shrugged, trying to push down the lump rising in my throat. *I had been gone too long.*

"And even prettier." Her gaze swept over me, slow and measuring, like she was checking for the damage she knew I hid behind my smile.

"I'm pretty sure you're legally required to say that as my grandmother," I said, smiling as she swatted at my arm.

"No." She shook her head as she slowly moved past me and toward the steps I had just climbed. "Some people have ugly grandbabies. That's just the truth of it." She waved her hand over her shoulder for me to follow her, but she didn't wait for me as she moved down the steps. "I was fortunate I didn't. I could never fake it."

"June!" I laughed as I trailed behind her.

"What?" She looked back at me with those amber eyes, and being with her felt like finding shelter in a storm. "It's the truth. Let's all say a prayer that your babies are pretty like you. If they aren't, I'd have to lie to the ladies at my book club, and you know how I feel about lying."

The old wood creaked as she leaned on the banister, but she still moved with purpose, even if she was slower these days.

She paused on the bottom step, glancing up at me. "Well? You comin'?"

Something loosened in my chest as I trailed behind her,

my feet remembering the path before my mind could catch up. "Where are we..."

But then I saw him.

He rose slowly, brushing his hands over his jeans, the sun catching on the sweat at the back of his neck. Heat flooded me until the only things I could focus on were the sound of my heartbeat and the sight of him. He shifted his weight, moving with the easy authority of a man who owned every inch of ground beneath his worn boots.

He looked carved from memory and like a stranger at the same time.

It didn't matter how much time had passed or how much he'd changed, seeing him was like a punch to the gut. I had left. I'd left because he'd told me to, and he was still here working away on his ranch, right next door to my grandmother's farm, as if he hadn't destroyed everything.

I took a small, instinctive step back, searching for something to hold on to, looking for anywhere to go but here. But then he turned, and I met his dark brown eyes. Eyes that didn't belong to the boy who'd broken my heart.

They belonged to his brother.

"Hunter." His name slipped past my lips, and he graced me with an easy, relaxed smile that seemed to light up his entire face as he wiped the sweat from his brow.

"Well, well, well," he drawled before he leaned against the fence. "Look what the cat dragged home."

His resemblance to Colt was like a physical blow.

Hunter was taller now, broader, his shoulders stretching the worn cotton of his T-shirt in a way they never had before. The lanky limbs and uncertain posture of Colt's younger brother had been carved clean away and replaced with a man with a chiseled jawline.

But the grin he flashed me over the fence was exactly as I remembered. One corner of his mouth hitched higher than the other, and a dimple appeared in his left cheek. It was the same smile I had watched him give girls to make their knees go weak, devilish in a way that promised trouble.

He swung open the gate that separated the two properties, boots crunching through the grass as he watched me.

"You're looking good, Blaire." He tipped his head in my direction, and I forced myself to stand straighter.

"Careful, Hunter. Compliment me too much and I might think you've missed me."

He laughed, and the sound curled through me. The deep rumble was warm and familiar in a way that made my skin prickle with warning.

He was far too similar to his brother.

"You wouldn't be wrong." His eyes traveled over me like he was taking inventory of the years between who I'd been and who I'd become. "We've all missed you. My mama still asks about you all the time."

I didn't answer. I couldn't.

I had missed them too, of course I had. Colt's family had once felt like where I belonged. His mother had been there for me when I'd lost my own, but they were little more than strangers now.

"Speaking of your mama, tell her I'll call her later once Blaire and I are settled," June said as she walked past him toward my car. "And make yourself useful and come carry her bags."

Hunter chuckled, but I quickly interjected. "You don't have to do that. I can manage."

"It's no trouble," he replied with a wink, lifting the hem

of his shirt to wipe his face. "It will give me a break from this damn fence."

I glanced at June as Hunter pulled both suitcases from the back seat like they weighed nothing.

"I don't know where I'd be without you Calloway boys." June patted his shoulder, and I quickly looked away. "You can drop them on the porch. We'll handle it from there."

"Yes, ma'am," Hunter replied before he moved past us and up the steps.

June was watching me with the smug assurance of someone who could read my thoughts like an open book, and her eyes twinkled with amusement.

"Don't even start," I warned as I pointed my finger at her.

She used to bring Colt up all the time after I left, and again, once she found out I was engaged to a man she called as useless as tits on a bull. But I always shut down conversations about him. I had wanted to know nothing about his life here. I couldn't handle it.

"Didn't say a word," she replied, her tone light and teasing, but she didn't press. She slipped her arm around my waist and guided me back up the porch steps. "We'll talk later," she whispered, her tone half affection and half warning.

Hunter lingered by the front door, one suitcase in each hand, as he waited for us. "You sure you don't want me to take these upstairs?"

"That's plenty, Hunter," June told him before grabbing the door. "I appreciate your help, you handsome thing."

A slow smile spread across his face, his cheeks flushing. "You're good for my ego, Ms. June."

"That ego doesn't need no help." She rolled her eyes. "Never has."

Hunter chuckled before he finally set down the suitcases and ducked his head. "You need anything at all, holler."

"Thanks, Hunter," I managed, as we walked into the house.

It smelled of old pine floorboards worn smooth by decades of footsteps, strawberries so ripe their sweetness hung thick in the air, and the faint trace of June's perfume.

It smelled exactly as I remembered, like home.

We rounded the corner into the kitchen, and there were baskets overflowing with vibrant berries that bled out onto the table. Some had juice seeping out and creating dark, sticky patches while others had shriveled like the forgotten casualties of a harvest too heavy for one woman to manage alone.

"Been busy around here. Shorthanded," June said casually, wiping her hands on her apron, though her eyes lingered on me.

My throat tightened with all the things I could say, should say, but I couldn't force the words out. Instead, I tied up my hair with unsteady fingers and grabbed the nearest basket, the wicker cutting into my palm.

"Where do you want me?" I asked, already scanning the room for the worst of the disaster.

She gave me a gentle smile, the one meant only for me, that used to heal every scraped knee and mend every broken heart, but even June's magic couldn't reach the fracture Colt left behind. "Why don't you unpack your bags and get some rest? All of this can wait."

I shook my head. I was far too anxious to sit still. "I'll unpack later. I want to help."

She pointed out the kitchen window toward the rows of strawberries, their ruby flesh glistening under the merciless Tennessee sun. "Need to save what we can before the heat turns 'em all to mush. My farm hands are picking as much as they can, but the harvest has been heavy this year."

I kissed her temple, my lips brushing against the wisps of silver hair that had escaped her braids and moved to the back door. The hinges protested with a long, rusty whine as I stepped outside.

"I'm glad you're back, baby," June called after me. "It doesn't matter what brought you. It just matters that you're home."

CHAPTER 3
BLAIRE

Heat shimmered over the rows of strawberries as I stared out over the farm.

I needed this: the dirt under my fingernails, the sun turning my shoulders pink, and the sweet taste of strawberries in my mouth as I ate them straight off the vine. I craved the purpose of it, to matter again to myself and this place.

June had a few farmhands, but not enough to keep up with the sprawling acres she stubbornly refused to scale back. Work piled up everywhere, work that June wouldn't have been handling all on her own if I hadn't left.

I was already mapping out all the projects I would tackle, but the berries came first. I gathered them quickly, my fingers moving on autopilot and staining red from the fruit.

Pluck, drop.

Pluck, toss out the bad fruit.

I'd feared I might have forgotten how, but my hands remembered. The repetitive motion calmed me in a way nothing else had since I packed up my life. I had gone to my dad's while I tried to sort things out this past week, but I'd known it was a bad idea.

Each berry that landed in the basket felt like a quiet act of defiance, a step away from the person I'd left behind in Raleigh. That girl had let herself be consumed by a man who looked good in a suit but couldn't hold on to a promise, even if he stitched it into his skin.

That girl had been so desperate to be wanted, she shrank herself down into someone easier. But here, with my knees pressed into the warm soil, my father and Grant seemed so insignificant. If it weren't for my phone vibrating in my pocket for the fifth time since I'd arrived at June's, I might not have thought of them at all.

They didn't matter. Not on this dirt.

I yanked the phone from my pocket. Seven missed calls from Grant and another two from my father's secretary. Voice mails stacked up, but I left them to rot. I had no interest in hearing what they had to say, not anymore.

I looked up and spotted Hunter casually leaning against the newly mended section of fence on his side of the property line. He held his gloves loosely in one hand, and he watched me like he didn't care that I caught him.

I shielded my eyes and shot him my best withering look, though it lacked bite after the last couple hours in the heat. Working on the farm did that. It bled the venom right out of me and left nothing but the soft underbelly I tried to keep hidden.

"Aren't you supposed to be working?" I called, and he grinned.

"If anyone asks, I'm on my break." He turned toward the driveway as tires crunched over gravel. "You've only been here a couple hours, and you're already killing yourself. Maybe you should take one too."

I wiped my hair out of my face, tracking a blue pickup as it made its way up to the house. "I think I've had a long enough break." I didn't mean from the work. "Don't you?"

He raised an eyebrow. "That's not—The farm isn't going anywhere. You've got time."

But I didn't.

Time felt like a debt I owed this place, one which kept growing interest while I was off pretending to belong somewhere else, only to come crawling back when it all fell apart.

Hunter watched the truck as it got closer to the house, then he pushed off the fence. He walked through the gate separating June's property from the Calloway's with the casual air of someone who had all day to do nothing but bother me.

"You going to ignore those calls forever?" He nodded toward my phone, still in my hand and vibrating once again.

I quickly hit the ignore button before I shoved it back in my pocket. "It's not important."

The blue truck came to a stop in front of June's house and idled in the small turnaround. The door swung open, and a woman jumped out. She bounded up the porch, her blonde hair half falling out of her messy bun.

Hunter stiffened beside me; his gaze snagged on her for a heartbeat too long before he dragged it away.

"Who is that?" I motioned to the woman as June walked out of the house to greet her.

"Huh?" Hunter muttered, looking out over the fields, avoiding her entirely.

She stood there, seemingly oblivious to our presence, her

attention on June as she threw her head back and laughed. The sun caught in her blonde hair, turning it almost white at the edges. She was effortlessly pretty in a way that made me self-conscious of the sweat dampening my shirt and the dirt caked under my fingernails.

"That girl you won't look at. Who is she?"

Hunter didn't answer right away. He ran his hand over the back of his neck and tilted it from one side to the next as if trying to ease his tension.

"That's Maggie Dawson," he replied, before quietly clearing his throat.

I quickly cycled through my memories, searching for the name, but came up blank. "Did she go to school with us?"

Hunter made a sound between a grunt and a sigh. "No. She moved here a few years ago. Runs the bakery on Main."

He glanced back in her direction for a few long seconds, his jaw clenched before he tore his gaze away.

"What's going on there?" I circled my finger between them, like I was connecting invisible dots in the air.

"There's nothing going on."

I raised a brow as I studied him. "You just stare at everyone like that?"

He let out a low whistle and shook his head. "What about you, Blaire?" His voice dropped low enough to land the jab. "Should we talk about your love life next?"

I laughed, but even I knew how hollow it sounded. "What love life?" I turned, moving down the row of strawberries.

"I've heard some things through the grapevine." His footsteps crunched behind me as he followed. "You've been gone, what? Ten years now?"

I kept my eyes fixed on the berries nestled among their thick leaves. "Shouldn't you be doing something?" I nodded toward his chestnut mare, who stood tethered to the fence post, watching us with liquid eyes that missed nothing. "Your horse looks thirsty."

"I'm just saying," he continued, his voice more careful now. "It's a little wild seeing you after all this time. Especially after the way you left, after you and Colt—"

"Don't." The word came out sharper than I intended.

Hunter stiffened, his hands stilling at his sides.

I turned to face him fully, tension crawling up my spine. "You want to talk about Colt?" I forced his name past my lips, the syllable catching in my throat. "Then do it over there on your property. Not mine."

Hunter blinked, taken aback, and for the first time, he looked like he regretted opening his mouth.

"You're gonna see him, you know?" The way he said it, resigned like he already saw the collision coming, made something hot twist beneath my ribs. "I don't know how long you're planning on staying, but there's no way around it."

"I'm not worried about him." The lie tasted bitter on my tongue as my pulse thrummed against my neck. "I'm back here for June and for this farm."

Hunter shifted, like he might say something else, but then Maggie's laugh rang out from the porch again and we both turned toward the sound.

June lifted a hand, beckoning us toward the porch. "Y'all going to stand out there all day? Blaire, there's someone I want you to meet."

I didn't move at first. Not until Hunter opened the gate that led out of the strawberry fields and held it, waiting. I slipped past him without a word, but he cleared his throat. "I'm going to get back to work."

But June ruined his plans. "Hunter, turn off Maggie's truck on your way up here, will ya?"

"Shit," Hunter mumbled under his breath, his shoulders tensing.

I snickered as he trudged toward the idling truck, kicking up little puffs of dust with each reluctant step.

I headed up the worn path to meet the girl who had reduced the always charming Hunter Calloway to a tense, distracted mess.

Maggie sat in one of the rocking chairs, long legs crossed and a glass of tea sweating in her hands. She glanced up as I made my way onto the porch, and the smile that spread across her face was warm and genuine.

"There she is." June wrapped her arm around mine, drawing me closer to the woman. "This is my granddaughter, Blaire. The one I've told you about."

Maggie stood and extended her hand. "I was beginning to think you were a myth."

I shook her hand, even as I winced. "More like a cautionary tale."

"Aren't we all?" Maggie laughed. "It's so nice to finally meet you after everything June's told me."

"Please don't believe everything she says." I dropped her hand and leaned back against the porch railing.

"Ms. June would never lie," Hunter huffed, shifting his weight onto the first step, his dusty boot scuffing against the weathered wood. His eyes darted from the porch to the fields beyond, then to Maggie for a fleeting second before fixing on some invisible point in the distance.

June dropped my arm and moved to him so she could pat his cheek. "That's because you're a sweet boy, Hunter."

Maggie scoffed, an unladylike sound that she immediately tried to muffle with her palm pressed against her lips, and I couldn't help but smile.

"Or he's full of shit." I shrugged. "Either one."

Maggie's laughter bubbled up. "I see you've met him before."

"Nice to see you too, Mags." Hunter clapped his hand across the porch post, rattling the lattice beneath.

"Always a pleasure, Calloway," Maggie quipped, though the glint in her eye suggested otherwise.

June gave Hunter's cheek one last pat before turning toward the door. "Let me grab your berries, darlin'. I've got them boxed and labeled in the cooler."

"Thanks, June." Maggie set her glass down with a soft clink on the porch railing as the screen door clicked shut behind my grandmother. Then she turned to me. "So, what brought you back to Tennessee?"

I hesitated, feeling the weight of Hunter's gaze on me. "Needed a change," I finally answered. *That was the understatement of the year.* "City life was getting old, and I missed this place."

Maggie didn't push me for more. She nodded as her fingers absentmindedly traced the fraying edge of her shorts. So I wasn't sure why I felt compelled to continue, but the words tumbled out.

"And there might've been a guy," I said, the admission lingering in the hot afternoon air.

A guy who turned out to be the opposite of what I should have wanted.

She laughed, and her nose scrunched. "Isn't there always?"

"Unfortunately." I looked over at Hunter and finally met his familiar brown eyes that had witnessed the rise and fall of Colt and me from the bleachers at football games to the late-night bonfires on the lake bank where our properties met. Hunter had been there through it all, a kid with a front-row seat to our tangled history.

"Well, we're glad you're here. June's been needing the help." Maggie's voice was warm and kind, but it made guilt dig its claws deeper into my chest. "And I know she's been dying to have you home. She talks about you like you hung the moon and stars over this farm."

"I'm glad I'm here too," I told her honestly. "I've been gone too long. I think the country air might do me some good."

"A girl needs time to remember who she is." She laughed as she crossed her arms, fingers digging into her elbows, and her gaze flickered to Hunter.

I recognized the look in her eyes, and I pitied her. I knew how easy it was to fall for a Calloway brother, how their slow smiles and calloused hands could undo a girl piece by piece, but I also knew how it felt to have your heart broken by them as well.

"What are you doing tonight?"

I blinked, surprised by her question. "Uh, probably unpacking."

"I'll make you a deal." She smiled at me, but her fingers tapped nervously against her thigh. "I'll help you unpack if you come with me to meet a few friends at The Dusty Spur."

I opened my mouth to decline, the refusal already forming on my tongue, but Hunter let out a dry snort.

Maggie tilted her head toward him. "Problem, Calloway?"

He leaned one broad shoulder against the porch post, arms folded loosely across his chest. "No problem. But there's no way you're going to convince this one to go to The Dusty Spur. She left the cowboy bars behind a long time ago."

I could feel something hot and rebellious stir inside me at his words, and I caught my reflection in the window. My hair was a mess of curls that Grant would never approve of, my shoulders were already a little red from the sun, and I looked more like myself than I had in a very long time.

"I'll go," I said, because I wanted to.

"Hell yeah." Maggie grinned and rubbed her hands together. "This is going to be so much fun."

I deserved to have fun.

"All right, let's get you unpacked, then get ready to go find you a cowboy to dance with." Maggie looked genuinely excited about this plan. "I'll run the strawberries by the bakery after. My apartment is right above it, and I can get ready in no time."

"I have no interest in any cowboys. I've sworn them off."

Hunter laughed again, but we both ignored him.

"Me too," Maggie said around her soft laughter. "But then they keep making more cowboys and I keep drinking tequila. It's exhausting."

I laughed, a little of my tension easing, and I decided right then and there that I liked this girl. I liked her enough that I was going back to The Dusty Spur with her when it was the last thing I should do.

Because the last time I'd stepped foot in The Dusty Spur I was still a teenager, and I was drunk on the feel of Colt and the shot of vodka he'd talked one of the men at the table next to us into buying.

But so much had changed since that night.

The neon beer signs of The Dusty Spur belonged to a different lifetime, one where my lips tasted of cherry Chap-Stick and *him*.

Hunter was right.

I had left cowboy bars behind, but I was tired of letting men like Grant with his control, my father with his disapproving frown, and even Colt Calloway with his broken promises decide who I got to be.

I would walk into that bar tonight and try not to flinch when every head turned. There would be whispers and questions I didn't want to answer, but for the first time in a long time, I couldn't bring myself to care.

I brushed the dirt off my jeans, squared my shoulders, and let the smallest smile curve along my lips as I met Maggie's eyes.

"I can't make any promises on the cowboys but count me in for the tequila."

The Calloway Ranch Series

Cowboy Casual
Available now!

Small Town Smokeshow
Coming May 12th, 2026
Preorder now!

JOIN US IN HOLLYWOOD!

Want first dibs on new releases, bonus scenes, exclusive giveaways, and behind-the-scenes updates?

Subscribe to my Newsletter!

Want to hang out where the real fun happens: early ARCs, spicy secrets, giveaways, and all the juicy gossip before anyone else?

Become a member of Hollywood!

ALSO BY HOLLY RENEE

The Calloway Ranch Series:

Cowboy Casual

Small Town Smokeshow

The Veiled Kingdom Series:

The Veiled Kingdom

The Hunted Heir

The Rivaled Crown

Stars and Shadows Series:

A Kingdom of Stars and Shadows

A Kingdom of Blood and Betrayal

A Kingdom of Venom and Vows

A Kingdom of Fire and Fate

The Good Girls Series:

Where Good Girls Go to Die

Where Bad Girls Go to Fall

Where Bad Boys are Ruined

The Boys of Clermont Bay Series:

The Touch of a Villain

The Fall of a God

The Taste of an Enemy

The Deceit of a Devil

The Seduction of Pretty Lies

The Temptation of Dirty Secrets

The Rock Bottom Series:

Trouble with the Guy Next Door

Trouble with the Hotshot Boss

Trouble with the Fake Boyfriend

The Wrong Prince Charming

ACKNOWLEDGMENTS

Thank you to all the readers and bloggers! There are so many books to choose from these days, and I am beyond grateful that you chose to spend your time reading mine!

Thank you to my family for your unending support.

Thank you to my entire team for all your help!

ABOUT THE AUTHOR

Holly Renee is a USA Today bestselling author of romance that crackles with tension, swoons with heat, and leaves readers giddy with delicious banter. Whether she's whisking you off to a moon-drenched fantasy kingdom or a Tennessee ranch filled with heartbreak and horses, her stories are fast-paced, emotionally charged, and undeniably fun.

Born and raised in East Tennessee, Holly is a married mom of two, a lake enthusiast, a lifelong lover of pink, and hopelessly obsessed with the kind of love that makes you scream into your pillow.

Find her at www.authorhollyrenee.com.